"Ka

Sean said, his voice sharp despite the endearment. "Stop tossing that word *friend* at me."

"But we are friends, we…"

"Katie," he warned. "Stop it, or—"

Her eyes went all dark and liquid. "Or what?" she asked in a voice that had gone as smoky as her eyes.

"Or I haul you into my lap and kiss you until I knock the socks off both of us."

"But we're supposed to be friends."

"Is friendship enough for you?" he asked.

Because right now friendship didn't seem nearly enough for him. Not when she was looking at him as though he was her fantasy come to life, the knight to slay her dragons. Not when he wanted to be the man to make her believe in fairy tales and magic again.…

Dear Reader,

Welcome to Silhouette Desire—where you're guaranteed powerful, passionate and provocative love stories that feature rugged heroes and spirited heroines who experience the full emotional intensity of falling in love!

Wonderful and ever-popular Annette Broadrick brings us September's MAN OF THE MONTH with *Lean, Mean & Lonesome*. Watch as a tough loner returns home to face the woman he walked away from but never forgot.

Our exciting continuity series TEXAS CATTLEMAN'S CLUB continues with *Cinderella's Tycoon* by Caroline Cross. Charismatic CEO Sterling Churchill marries a shy librarian pregnant with his sperm-bank baby—and finds love.

Proposition: Marriage is what rising star Eileen Wilks offers when the girl-next-door comes alive in the arms of an alpha hero. Beloved romance author Fayrene Preston makes her Desire debut with *The Barons of Texas: Tess,* featuring a beautiful heiress who falls in love with a sexy stranger. The popular theme BACHELORS & BABIES returns to Desire with Metsy Hingle's *Dad in Demand*. And Barbara McCauley's miniseries SECRETS! continues with the dramatic story of a mysterious millionaire in *Killian's Passion*.

So make a commitment to sensual love—treat yourself to all six September love stories from Silhouette Desire!

Enjoy!

Joan Marlow Golan
Senior Editor, Silhouette Desire

Please address questions and book requests to:
Silhouette Reader Service
U.S.: 3010 Walden Ave., P.O. Box 1325, Buffalo, NY 14269
Canadian: P.O. Box 609, Fort Erie, Ont. L2A 5X3

DAD IN DEMAND
METSY HINGLE

SILHOUETTE *Desire*®

Published by Silhouette Books
America's Publisher of Contemporary Romance

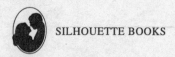 **SILHOUETTE BOOKS**

ISBN 0-373-76241-0

DAD IN DEMAND

Copyright © 1999 by Metsy Hingle

Visit us at www.romance.net

Printed in U.S.A.

METSY HINGLE

is a native of New Orleans who loves the city in which she grew up. She credits the charm of her birthplace, and her own French heritage, with instilling in her the desire to write. Married and the mother of four children, she believes in romance and happy endings. Becoming a Silhouette author is a long-cherished dream come true for Metsy, and one happy ending that she continues to celebrate with each new story she writes. She loves hearing from readers. Write to Metsy at P.O. Box 3224, Covington, LA 70433.

For Rita and James Hingle…Mom and Dad.
With love and thanks for their extraordinary son
and for the gift of their love.
Happy 60th Anniversary!

One

"**I**'m going to have a baby."

Sean Fitzpatrick's size-thirteen foot slipped off the desk, and he grabbed the arms of his chair to keep from sprawling onto the floor. Stunned, he stared at Katie Malloy—the woman who had been his buddy and his best pal for more years than he cared to count. "You're what?"

"I'm going to have a baby," she repeated calmly, looking just as innocent now as she had nearly twenty years ago—right before she'd fired that first snowball across the backyard fence and hit him between the shoulders.

She was yanking his chain. Had to be, Sean decided, and reached for his coffee. "Quit joking around, Malloy. I'm not buying it. You might want to try selling that line to Michael and Ryan," he told her, referring to his brothers and partners in the detective agency. "They're more gullible than me."

"But I'm *not* joking. I *am* going to have a baby. And I want to hire you to help me find the father."

Sean choked, sputtering coffee across the stack of files on his desk.

"Are you all right?" Katie asked, already around the desk and pounding his back.

"Yeah. Yeah, I'm okay. Stuff just went down the wrong way. You can stop beating me to death now," he muttered, feeling as though the air had been sucked right out of his lungs. He couldn't believe it, didn't want to believe it. Katie pregnant?

"You sure you're okay?"

"I'm fine," he said, and waved her back to her seat. While he mopped up the mess, he glanced at her and recognized that I-am-woman-I-can-do-anything look in her eyes. A sure sign of nerves. Sheesh! Of course she's nervous, Fitzpatrick. The poor kid's probably scared to death. Anger shot through him like a bullet, and he decided murder was too good for the guy who'd left her in the lurch.

"So, will you help me?"

"Don't worry. I'll find him." And when he did, he was going to take great pleasure in rearranging the jerk's face.

"I *knew* I could count on you," she said, giving him that million-dollar smile that always made him feel ten-feet tall.

"You'd better believe it." After all, Katie was practically family, had been almost from the time she and her mother moved to Chicago and bought the house next door to his parents. Katie had been a fixture at the Fitzpatricks' home from the moment she'd teamed up with his cousin Molly and pitted herself against the Fitzpatrick brothers. Except for a brief teenage crush he'd suspected she'd had on him, he and Katie had shared a friendship every bit as close and enduring as the one she shared with his cousin. Heck, they'd grown even closer since he'd moved into her apartment complex two years ago. He considered her his best friend.

And now Katie was pregnant. He could hardly believe it. The last he'd heard, she wasn't even dating anyone seriously. Sean frowned. At least, she hadn't been seeing anyone when he left town a month ago on that insurance fraud investigation. A lot could happen in a month, he reminded himself, as he glanced at her still-flat stomach. Obviously it had.

"You have no idea how relieved I am. I wasn't sure how you'd feel about helping me."

Sean snapped his gaze back to her face, stung that she'd doubted him. "You thought I wouldn't help? That I'd turn my back on you when you needed me?"

A haunted look came into her eyes. Old hurts, he guessed, thinking of her father's desertion, her stepfather leaving after the divorce, the turkeys who'd disappointed her, including the weasel who'd gotten her pregnant and then bailed. "You're right. I never should have doubted you, Sean. I'm sorry."

Feeling somewhat placated, his voice gentled as he said, "Just remember that I will *always* be here for you. All right?"

She nodded, then took a deep breath. "So, what kind of information do you need to get started?"

Sean paused a moment, searched for a way to delicately phrase the question he had to ask her. "I...um, before we get into that. Honey, are you sure about going through with this?"

"I'm positive. I've wanted a baby for ages."

Her decision didn't surprise him. Knowing Katie and how much she loved kids, he didn't really think she would consider terminating the pregnancy. But he'd had to make sure she knew there were options. "All right." Grabbing a pencil, he flipped to a clean sheet on his notepad. "The first thing I need is the name of the baby's father."

"Well, I'm not sure yet. I came up with five possibilities initially, but I've narrowed it down to three."

The pencil in Sean's fist snapped in two. He knew Katie could be reckless, even unpredictable, and he'd long suspected much of her bravado and bluff were her way of masking fear. But one thing Katie wasn't, was stupid. *Five* lovers? Katie?

She began digging in the monster-size bag she called a purse and pulled out a sheet of paper. "Here, I've written their names down for you."

Dumbfounded, Sean stared at the woman offering him a slip of paper with the names of her lovers. As a man, he truly enjoyed the opposite sex, and had yet to meet a woman who didn't garner at least a second glance from him. Because they were friends, he'd made a point of not giving Katie a second or even a third look. But he looked at Katie now—not as her friend, but as a man. She wasn't beautiful, not even pretty or cute. But pretty or not, a man couldn't help but notice those wide, whisky-colored eyes or think about removing the pins from those wild, not-quite-red, not-quite-brown curls she wore piled up on her head. Noting his own flexed fingers, Sean curled them into fists.

Katie rattled off something about lists and candidates, and he shifted his gaze to her mouth—proud and sassy, just like her. He felt a tug, low in his body, and acknowledged that this wasn't the first time he'd wondered about that mouth.

He skimmed his gaze down her body, noted the way her small breasts filled out the skinny white top, the way her narrow hips flared beneath the floral skirt. She was built on the thin side for his tastes, Sean admitted.

But damn if the woman didn't have showstopper legs. Those legs alone could be a source of real trouble for a man.

"So, I put together this list of possibilities."

She crossed those fantasy legs, and black lace winked at him. And Sean nearly swallowed his tongue. Trying to blot out the image of that black lace and the unholy thoughts it incited, he squeezed his eyes shut. Big mistake, he realized, because suddenly he had no trouble at all picturing Katie in bed—wearing nothing but that sin-black lace. Steamy sex and innocence, he decided, envisioning those long, slim legs of hers wrapped around his waist as she took him inside her.

"Sean? Are you okay?"

He slammed the brakes on his dangerous thoughts and snapped open his eyes. "I'm fine," he said, his voice gruff.

Get a grip, Fitzpatrick. This is Katie, remember? Katie— your buddy, your pal, practically your sister. She's the same pest who wore braces and pigtails, who annoyed the heck out of you as a kid. She's the brat who kept beaning you with snowballs until you pinned her down and kissed her because your mother said a guy couldn't hit a girl.

Only she *wasn't* his sister, and he had definitely not been thinking of her as his pal. Somewhere along the way, little Katie Malloy had traded in her braces and pigtails for the face of a temptress and a body designed to make a man sweat.

And he was sweating, Sean admitted, aware that his jeans had grown painfully snug. Annoyed with himself and with her for being the source of his discomfort, he scowled. "So, which one of the guys do you think is the father?"

Katie flicked her tongue across her bottom lip, a nervous habit he'd seen her employ a zillion times. Only this time the innocent gesture had him squirming in his seat. "I haven't made up my mind yet. That's why I'm here. I need your help so I can decide which one will make the best father.''

Sean's jaw dropped. He snapped his mouth shut and gave himself a mental shake. ''Back up a minute. Are you, or are you not pregnant?''

Katie blinked. ''Well, of course I'm not pregnant. At least not yet. That's why I'm here. I need your help.''

''What?''

''You thought— Oh!'' Suddenly she started laughing.

''This isn't funny, Malloy,'' he told her. He loved women, Katie included, but no way was he going to get himself tied down with one. At least, not yet. Maybe never, he amended.

''Sorry,'' she said, not looking the least bit repentant. ''It's just that your face...'' Another set of giggles sneaked out.

''Katie,'' he warned.

''Oh, for Pete's sake, Fitzpatrick, relax. I didn't mean you literally. I meant that once you've checked out my daddy candidates, I'll be able to make an intelligent decision about which one to ask to father my baby.''

Sean swore. ''Of all the dumb, idiotic—'' Biting off the rest, he stomped over to her, gripped the arms of her chair instead of her throat. He shoved himself in her face. Through gritted teeth he asked, ''And just what am I supposed to do? Act as your clearing house for sperm donors?''

''Don't be ridiculous,'' she said, meeting his angry glare. ''If all I wanted was a sperm donor, I would have gone to a sperm bank—not a detective agency. I intend to choose the man who's going to father my baby, not leave the decision up to chance.''

Sean swore again, then whirled away so he wouldn't

shake her as he wanted to do. Frustrated he prowled through his desk in search of his emergency stash of M&M's. He scooped up a fistful, and automatically held out his palm for Katie to fish out the yellow ones. After she had done so, he popped the rest of them into his mouth. "Not that I'm agreeing to anything, but just what is it you expect me to do?"

"Check out the candidates on my list." She waved the ivory sheet of paper in her hand. "You know, do a background check, sort of like the ones a company does when they're considering a potential employee."

Sean snorted. "Sweetheart, you've been sniffing way too many fingerpaints at that nursery school where you work."

Practically vibrating with indignity, she planted her hands on her hips and met his mocking gaze. "I'm serious, Sean. I want to hire you to investigate my daddy candidates."

"I've got a better idea. Save your money, and just have the poor saps fill out an application."

"I can do without your sarcasm."

"Better yet, try getting married first. You remember what marriage is, don't you? It's that old-fashioned thing that most people do before they decide to have a baby?"

Katie's cheeks flushed. Temper flashed in her eyes, making them glow like amber. "This is the nineties, Fitzpatrick. A woman doesn't have to get married anymore just to have a baby."

"Yeah? Well, maybe they should."

"It's not your decision. It's mine. And I've decided I want to have a baby." She held up her hand before he could object. "This is important to me, Sean. *Really* important. The most important thing I've ever done or probably will ever do in my life. I don't want to mess up and choose the wrong man. That means I need to learn as much as I can before I make a decision.''

"Fine," he told her, his own temper fraying. "Then have a D&B report run on the guys on your list. You'll get all the financial history you need."

Katie's lips thinned. "Who gives a flying fig about bank balances? I'm interested in finding out what's inside here." She poked her thumb at her heart. "We both know I don't have the best track record when it comes to men," she said, referring to her two broken engagements.

"So you had a couple of narrow escapes. You were too good for those clowns, anyway."

"Maybe. But I need to be sure the man I choose is someone who's going to stick around and be a loving and supportive parent."

Sean heard the echo of the lonely little girl she had been, the one who had been so hungry for a father's love and affection. It tore at him as nothing else she said could. It also made him want to spend ten minutes alone in a back alley with her father, her stepfather and every man who had ever let Katie down. Still, this idea of hers was crazy. He couldn't let her do it. "Honey, the guys on that list could all be saints, and I'd still think you were making a mistake. Are you really willing to undergo artificial insemination and have some guy's baby based on a PI report?"

"No, not exactly," she said sheepishly.

"Well, I'm relieved to hear that. You had me worried for—"

"My insurance won't cover artificial insemination. I'll have to get pregnant the, um, normal way."

"The normal way? You mean—" Sean swiped a hand down his face, tried to wipe out the sudden image of Katie in bed, her naked body tangled in satin sheets. Grateful for the shield the desk provided his lower body, he jerked his

X-rated thoughts back to the problem. Clawing a hand through his hair, he muttered. "Of all the dumb, lame-brained—"

The intercom on his desk buzzed. "Heather Harrison is on line two for you," his secretary told him. "She said it's about dinner tonight."

"Speaking of dumb—" Katie said.

"Tell her I'll call her back." He shot Katie a quelling glance and, using his most intimidating voice, he said, "I want you to forget about this crazy scheme of yours, Katie."

"I will not."

"I mean it," he insisted.

"So do I. And given your narrow-minded attitude," she said, her voice as stiff as her spine. "I can see I was right to scratch your name off my list."

"My— You had my name on that list!" He wasn't sure if he was angry or glad that she'd considered him.

"Obviously, I was desperate."

The crack scraped at him, fueled his temper. "What were you going to do? Knock on my door, and ask me if I'd mind sleeping with you so you could get pregnant?"

She hiked up her chin. "As a matter of fact, yes."

Don't go there, man.

But it was too late. An image jumped to life in his mind's eye—Katie lying beneath him, their bodies warm and damp from making love. The ache below his belt worsened. His sex strained against his jeans. Cursing the animal in him, Sean reminded himself that the woman he was lusting after was Katie—his friend.

"Don't sweat it, Fitzpatrick. You're off the hook. I'm not going to beg you to have sex with me," she said, her voice as icy as a Minnesota winter. "Like I said, I was feeling desperate at the time. Obviously, coming here today and asking you to help me was another mistake.''

She jammed the list into her purse and spun around, but not before he caught the flash of pain in her eyes. "Katie, wait. I didn't mean—''

The intercom buzzed again. "Get a move on, Sean,'' his brother Michael ordered. "Adam Stevens is here.''

"I'll be there in a minute." He blocked Katie's path. "If you'd just give me a second to explain…''

"No explanation is necessary. And I've changed my mind. I don't want to hire you. Now get out of my way.''

"No," he countered, angry with himself for being careless. It cut at him something awful to know he'd hurt her.

"Fine. Don't move. I will." Stepping around him, she moved past him and reached for the door.

"Aw, hell." Sean streaked in front of her, slapped the door shut and twisted the lock. Snagging her by the shoulders, he spun her around and pressed her spine against the door, trapping her between his outstretched arms. "You're not going anywhere until we settle this." He couldn't let Katie walk out now. If she did, he had a sick feeling that things would never be the same between them again. He didn't want to lose her.

"There's nothing to settle.''

The doorknob twisted. "Sean!" Michael pounded on the door. "Get your sorry rear out here. Stevens is cooling his heels in the conference room waiting to discuss his building's security.''

"I said I'd be there in a minute. Go ahead and start without me." Ignoring his brother's heated reply, Sean kept his eyes trained on Katie's face. "Look at me.''

When she failed to respond, he captured her face between his palms and more gently he said, "Look at me, Katie. Please.''

She shifted her gaze to his. There was anger simmering in the gold-flecked eyes. Anger. Pride. Hurt. Hurt he was responsible for, Sean acknowledged. His chest tightened with guilt, with regret. "I'm sorry."

"It doesn't matter—"

"It matters to me. I'd sooner cut off my arm than hurt you." And just as he'd done a hundred times before, he brushed his mouth against hers. It was meant to be a friendly kiss, a brotherly kiss between good pals. But heat licked through him like wildfire, setting his body and senses ablaze with desire. Awareness pulsed between them lightning quick. He watched her eyes soften, darken, and then he stopped thinking. He dipped his head again deepened the kiss. Her fingers curled into his shoulders as she parted her lips, and he dove in, wanting, needing to taste her. When her tongue found his, he groaned and pulled her closer.

A foot connected with the door, jolting them both. "Get your sorry butt out here now, Sean. Or I swear I'll kick this door in and wring your fool neck."

Sean lifted his head. His breath came in heavy rasps. So did hers. "I think he means it," she whispered.

"Yeah. So do I," he replied, and releasing her, he stepped back. Shock hit him first. Then panic streaked in. What in the devil was he doing? Coming on to Katie like this? Retrieving her purse where it had fallen to the floor, he eyed her warily. She looked dazed, nervous, aroused—exactly the way he felt. "Are we all right?" he asked, handing her the purse.

"Sure," she told him. But she looked ready to bolt. "You'd better go before Michael makes good on those threats. I'm sorry I bothered you."

"Listen, about this baby business..."

"Don't worry about it. I'll find somebody else to help me."

Damn! "Katie, I don't have time to argue now. Just promise me you won't do anything until we can talk."

"Really, Sean, I don't think—"

Michael beat at the door again, issued another string of threats. "Tonight. Just hold off on doing anything until then. We'll talk when I get home. I'll even bring pizza."

She hesitated.

"One with anchovies and a thick crust," he bribed.

"Anchovies?"

"Anchovies," he promised, no matter how much he detested the little suckers.

"All right."

He flipped the lock on the door, and Michael stormed in, angry enough to chew nails. "Excuse me, Katie, while I rip my idiot brother's head off."

"Rip away," she said. "I was just leaving."

Michael snarled at him. "I ought to knock your block off."

"Yeah? Well, stand in line," Sean muttered, irritated with himself. He had a sinking feeling that kissing Katie had been a major mistake.

Kissing Sean had been a mistake, Katie told herself for the umpteenth time. Gathering the ends of her hair, she secured it atop her head with a clip, then reached for the makeup bag. She coated her lashes with mascara, slashed the passion-pink lipstick across her too-wide mouth. For good measure she fastened on the pink sparkly earrings her stepfather had given her the Christmas before he'd split. Stepping back, she surveyed the results in the mirror of the dressing table in her bedroom.

Ordinary. Run-of-the-mill. Nothing special.

The words all but shouted at her like accusations. She stared at her heart-shaped face. Not one single feature stood out. Nothing about her stood out—except maybe her height. She cast a critical eye over the white blouse and cutoffs and sighed. Narrow curves on a five-foot, nine-inch frame might be great for models, but she felt like a scrawny chicken in a world full of peacocks.

Was that why no one in her life ever stayed? Because she wasn't pretty enough? Wasn't special enough? Wasn't lovable enough?

She thought of those petite blondes and redheads that breezed in and out of Sean's life—and no doubt his bed—women like Heather Harrison with her big blue eyes, chic blond hairstyle and double-D cups. Women who were nothing like her.

Not that she wanted to be one of Sean's women. Despite that ripple of sexual awareness that kept popping up between them, she'd decided long ago that Sean Fitzpatrick was out of her league. And while she'd made some real stinker decisions when it came to men, she wasn't fool enough to risk the kind of heartache a man like Sean would offer. Still a girl couldn't help but dream a little, and wonder how it would feel to be the one on the receiving end of that unholy grin or the wink of those deep blue eyes. It was easy to see why women fell for him. The man had enough charm and sex appeal to be declared a lethal weapon. If that kiss this afternoon was anything to go by, she was darn lucky she wasn't his type.

Kate shivered as she thought about that kiss again, recalled the feel of his mouth on hers, hot and demanding, the heat of his arousal pressed against her belly. He'd kissed her as though he'd wanted to swallow her whole. And for a few insane seconds she'd wanted him to.

Of course, he'd regretted the kiss almost immediately.

Opening her eyes, she smiled ruefully and turned away from the mirror to make her way to the living room. That was the trouble with knowing Sean so well, she mused. She'd sensed his panic at once. And he'd been so pitifully obvious in his attempt to put things back to normal between them. She'd almost laughed aloud. And probably would have if it hadn't hurt quite so much.

Plumping up one of the big throw pillows on the couch, she hugged it to herself for a moment. No question about it, Katie girl, kissing Sean was definitely a mistake. And one she'd be wise not to repeat.

Sean was her best friend. And she'd sooner walk barefoot through broken glass than humiliate them both by reading anything into that kiss. No way did she want to jeopardize their friendship. It was too important to her. He was too important.

So tonight she would share his pizza, reassure him that one teensy kiss, no matter how steamy, didn't mean a thing. Sean could go back to the Heather Harrison goddesses he preferred, and she...well, she'd deep-six all these yearnings that kiss had stirred inside her.

After flipping on a Leann Rimes CD, she set about lighting the candles scattered around the room. Her thoughts drifted back to her thirtieth birthday and her painful self-assessment. She'd finally faced the fact that she attracted men who were snakes—men who were incapable of making a commitment. A genetic flaw, no doubt, rooted in her foolish quest for a nonexistent Prince Charming. The admission had been brutal, but she'd done the smart thing—ditched her quest for a fairy-tale prince. No more searching and waiting for some white knight to fulfill her dreams. But the one thing she just hadn't been able to let go of was her dream to have a baby.

Mercy, how she ached for a baby of her own to love. As

long as she could remember, she'd looked forward to being a mother. It was the reason she'd gone into child care and worked at the nursery. She loved holding the little ones, loving them, caring for them, and she hated letting them go at the end of the day. She wanted a baby of her own— a child to cradle in her arms, to laugh with and sing to, to give all the love bursting inside her. She'd be a good mother, she promised herself. Her baby would never doubt for an instant that she loved him or her. And despite what Sean thought, her plan made perfect sense. Too bad she couldn't ask Sean to be the father. That would be perfect.

The sharp knock pulled Katie from her musings. Plastering a smile on her face, she opened the door. And as it always did when she was near Sean, her pulse picked up speed. He still wore the same faded jeans. The sleeves of his denim shirt had been rolled up to the elbows, displaying hard muscles bronzed by the sun. His black hair looked as though he'd rammed his fingers through it one time too many. But it was the turmoil in those blue eyes that made her heart kick. "Ah, the pizza man," she said, striving to be light.

"I'm sorry about the kiss."

So much for light, Katie thought with a sigh. "Okay," she replied and peeked inside the box. "You really did get anchovies." Taking the pizza from him, she started for the kitchen.

"I was out of line today, and I'm sorry," he told her as he followed her into the kitchen.

"All right," she acknowledged, as she set down the pizza, lifted the lid again and sniffed. "Hmm. This smells delicious, and I'm starved." She opened a drawer and pulled out a handful of napkins. "You want to get the plates?"

"It was a mistake," he told her, sounding anxious. He

grabbed two plates from the cabinet, placed them on the white wooden table. "It never should have happened."

"Whatever you say." She poured a glass of milk for herself and grabbed a beer from the refrigerator for him. "You want a mug?"

He snatched the milk and beer from her hands and set them down with a clunk. "Damn it, Katie. Have you heard a word I've said?"

"Every single one," she assured him. And each one had been a swipe to her heart. "You were out of line to kiss me. It was a mistake. It should never have happened, and you're sorry. That about cover it?" She didn't wait for him to answer. "Now, do you mind if we eat before the pizza gets cold?"

"Would you forget about the blasted pizza? I'm trying to apologize."

Katie sighed. "All right, Sean. Go ahead. Apologize."

"I'm sorry I took advantage of you today. I don't know what got into me…what I was thinking, to make a pass at you the way I did." Emotions swam in his eyes like a brewing storm. He jutted out his chin. "If you want to take a swing at me, go ahead. I deserve it."

She couldn't help herself. Katie laughed. The foolish man was really beating himself up over that kiss.

"I'm glad *you* find this amusing. I don't make a habit of forcing myself on a woman, or…or of taking advantage of one when she's vulnerable."

"Is that what you think happened?" she asked, temper sparking, not only because he was apologizing for kissing her, but because he thought she was some twit. "You think I'm some weak, simpering female who couldn't stop you from kissing me if I'd wanted to?"

"I think—"

"Well, think again, Fitzpatrick." She poked him in the

chest with her finger. "I am not one of your big-chested Cupie Dolls. You may have kissed me, but I kissed you back. You didn't take anything from me that I didn't want to give. Is that clear?"

"Crystal."

"Good. Now can we eat before this pizza turns to ice?"

"By all means. Eat. Maybe food will improve that sweet disposition of yours. Anyone ever tell you, you've got a nasty temper, Malloy?"

"I believe you've mentioned it a time or two." She brushed past him, flipped open the pizza box and dished out slices onto the plates. Sean said nothing as he took the seat across from her. But she could feel him watching her as they ate in silence. His assessing glances licked along her nerves. Finally, when she could stand it no longer, she dropped her pizza onto the plate. "All right. Out with it."

"What?" He reached for another slice of pizza.

"Don't give me that choirboy look, Fitzpatrick. I've known you too long to fall for it. Just spit out whatever it is that's got you sizing me up like a piece of evidence in one of your investigations."

He smiled. Slowly. Seductively. In a way that made her throat go dry. "I was just thinking about what you said. You know, how I didn't take anything that you didn't want to give?"

She narrowed her eyes. "So?"

"So, I couldn't help wondering…" His gaze dropped to her mouth, and Katie's heart started to gallop. "I was wondering if you provoked me deliberately this afternoon so I would kiss you."

"I provoked you?"

"Uh-huh. With all that crazy talk about needing me to help you find someone to get you pregnant."

"There's nothing crazy about it. And it wasn't just talk.

I intend to get pregnant. As for needing you to find me someone, I don't. I've already got three candidates. It's simply a matter of choosing the right one.'' She snitched a piece of bell pepper from his pizza and popped it into her mouth. ''And I don't need you to do the investigations for me, either, because I've decided to do them myself.''

''You? Lord, help us all.''

''Funny. Besides, how hard can it be? All I have to do is lift a few fingerprints, snag a wallet for credit card and driver's license numbers, maybe make a few phone calls to an employer or an old girlfriend.''

Sean shuddered. ''Quit clowning around, Katie. The thought of you playing Mata Hari sends chills down my spine.''

''You're a riot, Fitzpatrick, and I'm not kidding. I bet I'd make a good detective,'' she countered, warming to the idea.

''You'd be about as good at investigating as I'd be at running a nursery school.''

''Oh, I don't know,'' she said, tipping her head to the side. ''I bet the little girls would love you, and I think you'd look awfully cute changing diapers.''

''Don't hold your breath.''

She smiled at him. Finishing the last of her pizza slice, she licked her fingers clean.

''You're really determined to do this pregnancy thing?''

''Yes.''

''Then I'll do the investigations for you—on one condition.''

''What condition?'' she asked warily.

''If I come up with anything, and I do mean anything, that makes these so-called candidates unsuitable, you promise me that you'll forget the whole idea.''

Katie hesitated. The truth was that if none of her candidates panned out, she wasn't sure what she'd do. "I really do want to have a baby, Sean."

"That's the deal. Take it or leave it."

She hesitated. "If none of them pan out, I promise I'll rethink the idea. All right?"

He sighed. "Do I have any choice?"

Katie squealed. Jumping up, she ran over to Sean and threw her arms around his neck, then proceeded to cover his face with kisses. "Oh, thank you. Thank you. Thank you."

"Not that I mind having a woman throw herself at me, but you might want to hold off on a few of those thank-you kisses. You may not be happy with what I find."

"Oh, I will be. I know it."

"We'll see. Now where's the list?"

"I'll get it." Abandoning the kitchen, Katie dashed to her bedroom and retrieved the list from her purse. By the time she returned, he'd cleared away the pizza remains and was waiting in the living room. For a moment she allowed herself to just look at him. All six foot two inches of him were sprawled out on the couch, his head tipped back, his eyes closed. Lord, but the man was beautiful: those razor-sharp cheekbones; that stubborn jaw; the sexy mouth that could make a stone weep when he smiled, and turned her brain to mush with a kiss. The fact that the man had a good heart, a kind heart, made him darn-near perfect—everything a woman who believed in fairy tales could want. Except that she no longer believed in fairy tales, and even if she did, Sean would never see her as a princess.

As though sensing her scrutiny, Sean opened his eyes and stared at her. Awareness stirred, sparked between them, charging the air with tension, just as it had earlier. "Here's the list," she said, walking over to him.

His fingers brushed her palm as he took the sheet of

paper, and she fought back a shiver. Katie pressed her hand to her jittery stomach. "Those are the names," she said as evenly as possible. "And of course, I can give you whatever personal information I have. The first one, Eric, he's a salesman who—"

Suddenly Sean's shoulders stiffened. He shot his gaze back to her face. His eyes were dark and stormy. "What is it? What's wrong?"

"You put Michael's name on this list?"

"Well, yes. Initially," she said, confused by his accusing tone. "I told you, I started off with five names and narrowed it down to three. You and Michael were the two I scratched."

"You actually considered sleeping with my brother?"

"Well, I can't say that I thought of it in quite those terms. But, yes, I guess I did. I mean if Michael had been the man I selected, then I would have…um…made love with him to get pregnant."

"I'm surprised you didn't put Ryan's and Connor's names on here, too," he snapped, referring to his two other brothers.

"Ryan's married and I draw the line at married men. But if I knew where Connor was, you can bet I'd have included him." Temper drove her, loosened her tongue. "Besides if Connor kisses anything like you and Michael, I imagine making love with him would be a pleasant prospect."

"Like me and Mich—" His eyes narrowed to angry slits. "You kissed Michael?"

"Not that it's any of your business, but yes. Michael and I kissed a number of times while we were dating."

Sean shot to his feet. "I don't believe this. You've been dating…kissing my brother?"

"Yes," she said sweetly, furious with him for finding

the idea so shocking. "Why? Is there some reason I shouldn't?"

"You're damned right there's a reason. He's...he's—"

"He's my friend. Just like you're supposed to be. But unlike you, Michael doesn't kiss me, then turn around and insult me by apologizing for doing it."

Two

"Hey, Bro," Michael said, replacing the telephone receiver on its cradle as Sean marched into his office. "I was just getting ready to buzz you with the good news. We got the Stevens' contract."

Sean slammed the door shut and stormed over to Michael's desk. Planting his palms on the polished mahogany surface, he leaned over and glared at his brother. "I ought to take your head off."

Michael arched his brow, sat back in his chair and gave him that cool, calm, lawyer look that drove Sean nuts. "You're welcome to try, little brother. But before I wipe up the floor with you, you want to tell me what you're so all fired up about?"

The anger that had been churning inside him since Katie had dropped her little bombshell about her and Michael the previous night kicked up another notch. "Where in the hell do you get off hitting on Katie?"

"Katie?"

"Yeah. Katie Malloy," Sean told him through gritted teeth. "You know, the skinny redhead with the smart mouth that we've known since we were kids?"

"Ah…that Katie."

At the smile spreading across his brother's mouth, Sean had to check the urge to grab him by his designer shirtfront and wrap the fancy tie around his throat.

"I'm not sure if I'd call a handful of dates 'hitting' on her, but Katie and I have gone out together a few times. What about it?"

"You think just because you buy her a couple of meals that gives you the right to jump her bones?"

The smile on Michael's lips died faster than a snap. "Who said I jumped her bones?" Michael demanded, fists ready. "All I did was kiss her a few times."

Discovering that there had been more than one kiss did nothing to cool Sean's already-hot temper. "So you admit it. You've been putting the moves on her."

"I'm not admitting anything." Eyes narrowed, Michael eased back into his seat. "Not that it's any of your business, but I hardly think that sharing a few kisses—in which, I might add, Katie was a willing participant—constitutes my 'putting the moves' on her. At least not in my book, it doesn't."

Sean hadn't wanted to believe it, that Katie really was involved with his brother. After she'd all but thrown him out last night, he'd spent most of it lying awake, chewing on what she'd told him. He'd decided to have it out with her first thing this morning. Only it had been after four when he'd finally dozed off, and by the time he'd awakened with a splitting headache, Katie had already left for work. To make matters worse, he'd had a full hour to let the steam build while he'd waited for Michael to arrive at the office.

His brother's confirmation that he and Katie did indeed have a more personal relationship left a bitter taste in his mouth. "What's the matter? Aren't there enough other women in this city for you to hit on without going after Katie?"

Michael clenched his jaw. "Listen, pal. Who I go out with is none of your business. You don't see me giving you grief about the women who parade in and out of your apartment, do you?"

"None of those women is Katie."

Fingers steepled, Michael gave him a considering look. "Is that the problem? Katie turn you down?"

Sean made a suggestion as to what his brother could do with himself.

"Hit a nerve, did I?" Michael taunted.

Sean swore and cast aspersions on the nature of his brother's parentage.

"Before you go through your limited vocabulary, you might want to remember that the two of us are brothers—which means we share the same parents."

"Don't remind me."

"So, you going to tell me why my going out with Katie has steam coming out of your ears? Or you want me to guess?"

"You know what you can do with your guesses," Sean told him.

"Could it be that after all these years, you've developed a case of the hots for Katie yourself?"

"Katie and I are friends," Sean snapped, clenching his hands into fists at his side. But the memory of the kiss they'd shared yesterday loomed before him. It was a fluke, Sean told himself, brought on by a bout of celibacy and the fact that Heather had been playing games with him, putting him off. He and Katie were just friends. "I'm angry because Katie's...she's practically family, and you putting the moves on her isn't right.''

"Now that is dumb. Katie may seem like family because we've all known her a long time, but there's no blood tie to prevent either of us from becoming involved if we want to.''

Involved. The word gnawed at him. "Just cut all the BS and tell me, are you serious about her?''

"Why? You worried about competition?''

Sean snorted. "You really are full of it, Bro. Believe me, if I were interested in Katie, you wouldn't be any competition. I already told you, she and I are friends. That's all.''

"Uh-huh.''

Michael's smug expression only infuriated him more. "I don't want to see her get hurt. All right?''

"And what makes you think I'm going to hurt her?''

"Because...because she's not your type.''

"I don't have a type,'' Michael informed him. "And if I did, why not Katie? She's an interesting woman, fun to be with, and she makes me laugh.''

Katie was all those things, but hearing Michael say it sent uneasiness clawing down his spine. "So, you saying you are serious about her?''

The lengthy silence caused a tight, funny feeling in Sean's chest. "I thought about it,'' Michael admitted. "And I suspect Katie did, too. But whatever it is that makes two people want to share their lives together, wasn't there for us. Katie and I pretty much agreed we'd just stay friends.''

Relief flooded through Sean. His heart made its way back down his throat. But when he glanced at Michael, saw his grin, temper pricked at him. "Why you son of a—'' He bit off the rest. "Why didn't you just say so to begin with?''

"Because it was a lot more fun watching you tie yourself up in knots over the idea of me being with Katie."

"Go to hell," Sean told him. "I've got work to do." Whirling around, he stomped out of Michael's office and headed for his own.

Ten minutes later Sean studied the information he had gathered on an investigation he was working that involved a child kidnapping. As he studied a picture of the mother and daughter, images of Katie sneaked into his thoughts. Katie telling him she wanted a baby, that she planned to get pregnant. Katie with her face flushed, her lips swollen, those whisky-colored eyes of hers filled with yearning and need. The kiss yesterday had been a fluke, Sean told himself again. He wanted, needed, desperately to believe that—for his sake and Katie's.

The intercom buzzed. "Heather Harrison is on line three."

He grabbed the phone, eager to chase these crazy thoughts about Katie from his mind. "Heather, darling," he said, crooking the phone between his shoulder and ear. For the next few minutes he listened to the shapely blonde he'd lusted after for the past three months. But when he hung up the phone with a promise to get back to her later, it wasn't the voluptuous blonde with the sexy blue eyes whose face kept stealing into his thoughts. It was a skinny redhead with vulnerable, whisky-colored eyes.

That same skinny redhead was still in his thoughts that evening when Sean heard the knock at his door. "Door's open," he called out from the back deck where he'd set up the grill for barbecuing. Once he'd called and apologized to Katie for overreacting the previous night, he'd spent the better part of the day trying to make sense out of his sudden and unwise attraction to her. He'd come to the same conclusion each time. The kiss and his reaction to Katie had been a fluke. Having her over for a belated birthday dinner would prove it to himself and to her.

So much for his fluke theory, Sean decided when he glanced up and spotted Katie standing in the doorway. His senses went on full alert, like a fox scenting prey. The "friends only" mantra he'd been practicing all afternoon bit the dust the moment he saw her. Wearing a pink top tied beneath her small breasts and white cutoffs, she was not dressed to inspire lust. But one look at those Rockette legs, with the tips of her toes painted the same shade of pink as her worrisome mouth, and he was in trouble. The fact that she was looking at him—as if she'd just as soon skip dinner and have him for dessert—had his blood pressure hiking up, right along with another part of his anatomy. How in the devil was he supposed to think of Katie as his pal when his blasted hormones kept ambushing him?

She walked over to him—no sauntering, no slow swaying of her hips to entice—just a graceful, fluid stride that was all the more enticing because it wasn't meant to be.

"Hi." As always, she gave him a quick smack on the lips in greeting as though she didn't even remember that yesterday those same lips had rubbed against his, opened and tasted him like a welcoming lover. The friendly kiss was over in an instant, but it had been long enough for him to catch the scent of her perfume. Since when had the scent of honeysuckle become such an aphrodisiac?

"I wasn't sure what you were serving, so I brought red and white," she said, indicating the bottles of wine in her hands.

Sean wrapped his fists around the wine to keep himself from reaching for her. He checked out the labels. "Hey, these are both good. Your taste in wine is improving, Malloy."

"Gee. You have such a way with compliments, Fitzpatrick. If a girl isn't careful, you'll just turn her head."

Sean chuckled as he was meant to do, and the tension in him eased a notch. "We're having steaks. So, I'll open the red and let it breathe. Have a seat. I'll be right back."

"Need any help?"

"Are you kidding? You think I'd let you come near my kitchen again? It took me a week to rid the place of the stench of burned pasta." At her scowl, he laughed. "Go ahead, kick your feet back and relax. I've got everything under control."

And he did have everything under control, Sean told himself, as he poured more wine into their glasses. Claiming the chair opposite the old-fashioned porch swing where Katie sat, he congratulated himself. Everything had gone like clockwork—right down to the antique music box he'd given her as a gift.

It had been just like old times—comfortable, enjoyable. So what if he couldn't help noticing how soft her skin looked in the moonlight? Or the way her eyes sparkled when she laughed?

She looked up at him over the lid of the music box. "It's beautiful," she whispered in that throaty whisper that sparked visions of her lying on satin sheets. Quickly, ruthlessly, he deep-sixed the dangerous image.

"I'm sorry it's late," he told her.

"Don't be silly. You were out of town for my birthday. I know that. And you really didn't have to buy me anything. I got the most gorgeous bouquet of flowers from all the Fitzpatricks."

Sean shrugged, his gaze riveted to the fingers lazily stroking the silver latch on the music box. "The flowers were from my family," he said dragging his eyes up to her face. "I wanted to give you something from me."

"I...thank you."

The friendly sass that had been in her eyes all evening gave way to a soft yearning that made his blood heat. Desire, tucked safely away throughout dinner, sneaked out, tempting him. Sean tightened his grip on the glass in his hand and stood. "How about some more wine?"

"No, thanks," Katie told him, and carefully placed the music box on the table amid the nest of wrappings. Then she stood and went to him. Reaching out, she stroked his cheek. "Thank you, Sean," she whispered, then pressed her mouth to his. It was a simple kiss, over almost before it began, but it sent desire shooting through him like heat lightning. "I'll treasure it always."

She backed away, retreating until she came up against the swing and sat down. Not until she'd pushed off on her back foot and set the swing to swaying was he finally able to untangle his tongue.

The silence stretched between them for several awkward moments, then Katie cut him a narrow-eyed glance. "You know, Fitzpatrick, it just occurred to me that this dinner and that music box might actually be a bribe."

"A bribe, huh?" he said, welcoming the teasing and the break in tension that came with it. "And just what would I be bribing you for, Malloy?"

"Well, knowing what a sneaky man you are, maybe you thought that if you plied me with a great dinner, let me stuff myself with that sinful cake and gave me such a fabulous gift, that maybe I'd let you off the hook about doing the investigations for me like you promised."

"The thought never crossed my mind."

"That's good. Because I'm not letting you off the hook, pal."

Try as he might, he couldn't sustain the light humor. "Katie, about this baby business—"

"Tonight when you lit the candles on the cake and told me to make a wish, do you know what I wished for? I wished that by this time next year, I'd have a baby. I know you don't agree with this, Sean, but as long as I can remember, I've wanted that package. You know—husband, wife, babies—a family. A psychologist would probably say it's because I didn't have the family I wanted as a child with my parents divorcing, my stepfather cutting out on us and stuff. And they'd probably be right. But I always knew that someday I would have a family like...well, like yours."

She tore at the napkin in her fingers. "Well, it hasn't happened, and it isn't going to—at least not the husband part of it. But I still want the babies, Sean. Sometimes I think it was because I wanted to have children so much that I talked myself into thinking I was in love and getting engaged twice. I think I wanted to get married so I could become a mother."

It broke his heart to hear the sadness in her voice, to see it in her eyes. Family was something that he'd always taken for granted, and it was something that Katie had never really had. Sean put down his wineglass. "Honey, I understand what you're saying. But—"

"You don't agree with me on this. I know that, and I understand. Really, I do. But I know what I'm doing, Sean."

Frustration knotted like a fist in his stomach. "You're a young woman, Katie. You deserve more than stud service from some guy who'll be happy to get you pregnant and then more than likely split on you. You deserve the whole shebang—love, marriage, babies, white picket fences."

"You're talking about fairy tales. I stopped believing in them and in Prince Charming a long time ago."

"Maybe you just haven't found your prince yet."

She gave him a smile that was meant to be cocky, but came across as impossibly sad. "Believe me, I've kissed my share of frogs, even got engaged to two of them, remember? But not one of them ever turned into a prince. I don't want—no, I refuse to put my life on hold and wait for someone who probably doesn't exist."

There was an aching loneliness in her voice that ripped at him. "Whatever happened to that little girl? The one who believed in knights and fairy tales and magic?"

"She grew up."

And because she had grown up, she knew not to read anything into the sexual voltage that kept zinging between her and Sean. Oh, it had always been there on her part. It was pretty hard not to have fantasies about a man like Sean. But fantasies were all that they were. She'd gotten used to feeling that heat suck low in her belly every time he was near her, and she'd gotten good at hiding it from him. So what if he seriously kissed her a time or two—she was too smart to let that romantic heart of hers start spinning fairy tales again. Sean wasn't interested in her in that way. He was simply being a good friend.

And it was out of friendship, she knew, that he was still trying to talk her out of her plans to have a baby thirty minutes later.

"I don't like it, Katie," Sean told her as he paced to the end of the deck. "Not one bit."

"You've made that pretty clear—more than once already." Katie released a weary sigh. "But whether you like it or not doesn't matter. I'm going to do this—with or without your help. Just tell me whether I need to find someone else to handle the investigations or not."

"I said I'd do it, didn't I?" he snapped, coming to a halt in front of her. "Where's the list?"

She retrieved the slip of paper from the pocket of her shorts, unfolded it and handed it to him. He glared at the names a moment, then straddled the chair next to her. ''All right. Tell me everything you can about each of these guys.''

A glass of wine later, Katie leaned back against the patio chair. ''That's about it. At least, it's everything I know.''

Sean scowled at the notes he'd made next to the names on her list, then glanced up and fixed her with stormy blue eyes. ''It's not a hell of a lot—especially considering what you're planning. The longest you've known any of these guys is six months.''

''Sean,'' she said, a warning in her voice.

''All right. All right.''

''Is it enough for you to work with?''

''I guess it'll have to be, won't it?''

She refused to justify her decision to him again. Besides, even if she were to try to explain, she doubted Sean would understand. She didn't want to be disappointed again or to be the one to disappoint. So, why couldn't Sean accept that? ''Can you do the investigations with the information I've given you? Or do I need to try to get social security or driver's license numbers?''

''And suppose I do need those things, how did you plan to get them? By swiping wallets like you threatened?''

Katie flinched at the derision in his tone. Hurt, angry, she snatched the list from him and stood. ''Just forget it. I was right yesterday. I never should have asked you to help me in the first place.''

''Aw, hell!'' He caught her by the wrist before she'd taken two steps. ''I'm sorry,'' he told her.

When she didn't reply, he sighed. ''Give me back the list,'' he urged, holding out his hand. When she didn't respond, he plucked the sheet of paper from her fingers. But instead of releasing her, he led her over to the swing and sat down. When she remained stiff and unyielding, he said, "Come on. Sit with me. Just for a minute."

She continued to stand. So he tugged, pulling her down beside him. Then he set the swing in motion. "A lot of the stuff in an investigation like this is basic, and I'll be able to get a good part of what I need from public records," he explained. "I'll access most of the data with my computer. The internet is amazing. I've also got some contacts with the DMV and the police department that I can use to check for driving violations, complaints, outstanding arrest warrants, and stuff like that."

Hearing him talk about arrest warrants and police records sent a chill of uneasiness down Katie's spine. She brought her free hand to her throat. She couldn't imagine any of the men she was considering as a father for her child or for that matter any man she even dated, being a criminal. True, she hadn't known them long and only dated them casually. But each man had been a gentleman with a responsible job and had been a pleasant and companionable date. Each claimed to like children, and from the talks and discussions that they had shared, she'd learned that each man shared her views about raising a child. In short, on the surface each candidate appeared to be ideal daddy material.

Sean jammed the slip of paper into his shirt pocket. "I've got enough here to get started, so I don't want you to even think about playing Mata Hari. Okay?"

"All right."

Shoving off with his foot, he gave the swing another push and sent them swaying in a slow, languid motion. Still holding her wrist, his thumb moved in small, lazy circles over the inside of her wrist, causing her pulse to scatter. The sun had long since slid from the sky. Stars dotted the heavens, creating thousands of pinpoints of light. Moon-light spilled over the deck, enveloping them in its soft glow.

"H-how long will it take you to run the background checks?" she asked, and nearly cringed at how husky her voice sounded.

"The basics won't take long at all. But making inquiries about a man's character, especially discreet ones, isn't al-ways easy or fast."

"I know what I'm asking isn't easy," she said, turning her head to look at him.

"But not too hard." His lips curved into a slow smile that made her ache. "I guess it would have been a lot simpler for both of us if you'd just left my name on the list, huh? At least you already know all the secrets in my closet."

He dropped his gaze to her mouth, and butterflies started a dance in her stomach.

Maybe the sparks flowing between them all evening hadn't been exactly one-sided. And maybe she hadn't imagined the leap of desire in his eyes when he watched her. And maybe she had better just put a lid on these fan-tasies. Somehow Katie managed to laugh. "If that's your not-so-subtle way of offering yourself so that you can get out of doing the investigations, you can forget it, pal. I'm not buying it."

"No?" He released her hand and eased his arm around her shoulders in a move so smooth she barely noticed it until his fingers began to stroke her bare arm.

"No," she whispered.

The swing slowed to a stop. The fingers on her arm had somehow managed to find their way to the back of her neck, where they were working their way up her nape. "Why not?"

"Because…because we're friends."

Sean's fingers sieved through her hair, urging her closer. Katie's breath hitched. She pressed a hand against his chest, where his heart beat beneath her fingers faster than a stockbroker's tape. "Sean, I don't think this is a good idea."

"You're right. It's a lousy idea," he told her, his breath a whisper against her lips. "In fact, it's a flat-out crazy idea. No way should we do this."

"I agree," she murmured.

But knowing they shouldn't do this didn't seem quite enough. Katie didn't know which of them moved first, but suddenly Sean's mouth was on hers—touching, tasting, taking. All the warnings she had been repeating to herself since he had kissed her the last time simply flew out the window—along with her common sense.

When that first soft kiss deepened, then slid into another kiss and deepened yet again, the blood fired in her veins, and Katie could have sworn she heard bells ringing. Sean wrapped his arms around her while his tongue tempted and teased her to open the seam of her lips, dared her to taste him.

She took the dare. He moaned, a hungry sound of need that sent ripples of pleasure sluicing through her bloodstream. She clung to him as he dove deeper for another taste. Her tongue tangled, danced with his. He tasted like wine, sharp and earthy, like chocolate, smooth and sweet. He tasted like danger and sin. He tasted like magic and dreams. He tasted like Sean. No one could taste like him. No one else could make her feel as he did.

She heard the bells ringing again and reminded herself that she'd given up on wedding dreams. This was Sean—not some prince or white knight come to rescue her from loneliness. She was his friend—not some beautiful princess or damsel in distress who needed rescuing. It was hormones, the moonlight, the wine that had him kissing her like he wanted her, like he needed her, like there was no one else in the world for him but her. She wasn't Sean's type, never had been, never would be. She was a smart woman, too smart to believe that any of those things had changed, too smart to let this go on any longer.

But then his hands ran up and down her spine, sending delicious sensations climbing through her, and her traitorous body refused to listen to her at all. Instead she moved closer, asked for more.

He gave her more, kissing her deeper still. When he crushed her to him, pressed his hardness against her, she heard the blasted bells ringing again.

Sean lifted his head, said her name on a groan. Her body was vibrating with desire. She felt like she'd just weathered a tornado and was willing to try it again. Her eyes still closed, she simply held on to him. Thank heavens the ringing bells had stopped, she thought, as she opened her eyes and looked at him.

He cradled her face in his hands, and in the moonlight his eyes were black with need. "Katie," he whispered against her mouth.

"Sean?"

Katie's heart slammed to a stop at the sound of a female voice calling his name.

"Sean, honey? It's Heather."

Three

Sean made a strangled noise in his throat at the sound of Heather's voice. Talk about timing. A shudder went through him. The clip had disappeared from Katie's hair, leaving thick auburn curls falling about her neck and shoulders. Her cheeks were flushed, her eyes soft and dreamy. The pink lipstick on that troublesome mouth of hers was gone. She looked like a woman who'd just tumbled out of a man's bed. The thought sent another jolt of desire knifing through him. Somehow sanity reared its head, and he gripped her by the shoulders and set her away. "Good Lord, what am I doing?"

Katie stiffened beneath his hands, but he didn't let her go. Drawing another deep breath, he struggled for control. What on earth was he thinking? This was Katie. Katie!

"Sean?" Heather called out again, her voice closer.

"I'm sorry." He cringed the moment the words were out, but it was too late to take them back. "What I mean is I didn't plan for that to happen. I don't know what came over me. Or why I—''

"It's okay," she said, scrambling off the swing.

"It's not okay." And it wasn't. Even with only the light of the moon and the deck to aid him, he couldn't miss the color staining her cheeks, or the way panic had stolen into her eyes. Sean stood and caught her arm as much to steady her as to stop her from running. Because she was poised to run.

"Guess that's what we get for drinking all that wine," she said, in a voice as forced as the smile on her lips.

"I'm not sure we can blame the wine. I—''

"There you are," Heather said breezing through the doorway and out onto the deck with a foil-wrapped dish in her hands. "I rang the bell, but you didn't answer. Then I saw your truck, and decided to try the door. I thought I'd take a chance and drop by. I never did hear back from you today," she accused.

"I, um, I'm sorry. I got tied up."

"Well, I guess I'll forgive you this time," Heather said, a pouty look on her face, her thick lashes sweeping down over her baby blue eyes. She swished and swayed her way over to him. "Oh, hello, Katie," she said, barely sparing Katie a glance. "Would you be a sweetie and hold this for me while I tell this fellow hello?"

Not saying a word, Katie took the dish from Heather and turned away.

His eyes on Katie's retreating back, Sean barely heard Heather say, "I've missed you," before she had her mouth locked on his.

Removing Heather's arms from around his neck, Sean cut the kiss short, which apparently didn't please Heather, but didn't stop her from launching into a litany about her busy schedule. Sean tuned her out. How was it possible that for the past three months the voluptuous blond aerobics instructor had inspired such lust in him? Looking at her now, in the barely there, white shorts and cropped T-shirt that clearly displayed her ample assets, left him cold. Yet looking at Katie with her long legs and skinny curves had him breaking out in a sweat. It didn't make a lick of sense.

"Sounds like you really have been busy," Katie said.

"Oh, I have." Heather slid her gaze over to Katie who stood next to the table where she had placed Heather's dish. "How have you been?"

"Fine. I see you're looking fit as usual."

"Thanks. I'm conducting six classes a week at the body gym now. You should think about coming. I have one class where we work on muscle tone. You might find a toning class would help you fill out a bit."

"I'll think about it," Katie said, but Sean could have strangled Heather for the remark. What was wrong with a narrow torso and lean curves? They certainly suited Katie.

"Oh, my," Heather said, spying the wine and cake plates on the table. "I hope I'm not interrupting anything."

"As a matter of fact, Katie and I were having dinner," Sean told her.

"Oh," Heather replied, another pretty pout forming on her lips. She slanted a glance to the foil-covered dish on the table. "I didn't realize you'd made plans. I brought you one of my veggie casseroles. I'd hoped we could share it."

"Actually, we finished dinner a while ago," Katie informed her. "And you know Sean...the man's always hungry. He's probably ready for a snack already, and the casserole sounds wonderful."

Heather beamed. "It is very good, even if I do say so myself."

"Well, I'll just get out of your way and give the two of you some privacy." Katie began gathering the wrapping paper and ribbon and stuffing it into the box that had held her gift.

"You don't have to rush off," he said.

"I'm not rushing off. I've been here all evening, and I'm sure you and Heather have some catching up to do. But thanks, anyway. Dinner was great, and the gift is beautiful."

"Gift?" Heather repeated. Suddenly alert, her eyes darted like a laser to the music box Katie was carefully packing away. "Sean gave you a gift?"

Katie looked up. "Yes. A music box for my birthday."

"How sweet," the blonde said, relaxing. "You're lucky. My brother never remembers my birthday."

"I'm not Katie's brother," Sean informed her, for some reason irritated by the comment.

"Oh, I know that. But the two of you are such good friends, and you told me yourself how you practically grew up together. You're almost like brother and sister."

"I really do have to go," Katie said.

"No, you don't." At both women's surprised expressions, Sean said more calmly, "I mean, I'm sure there's enough of Heather's casserole for the three of us."

"Thanks. But I'm stuffed, and I've got a busy day tomorrow. I was planning to turn in early tonight."

"It's not even nine o'clock," Sean argued, ignoring Heather's obvious displeasure at his reluctance to have Katie leave. He sensed Katie's awkwardness and wasn't sure if it was because of Heather or the kiss. Somehow things had gotten all mixed up again, and he wanted to straighten them out.

"I know it's early, but I'm really tired. It's been a long day, and tomorrow's going to be even longer."

"Don't worry, we understand," Heather told her, linking

her arm through Sean's. "It was nice seeing you again, Katie. Oh, and happy birthday."

"Thanks." Katie barely spared Sean a glance as she said, "Don't worry about seeing me out. I know the way."

"Excuse me," Sean said to Heather and followed Katie to the door. "We still have a few things to go over regarding that matter we were discussing," he told her, aware that Heather had followed him and was eyeing the exchange from a short distance.

"Um, why don't you just give me a call and let me know what else you need? If I'm not home, you can leave a message, and I'll get back to you."

"What about the rest of your cake? Don't you want it?" he asked, barely able to keep the irritation from his voice.

She didn't even bother turning around to look at him. "Why don't you and Heather finish it?"

"Katie…"

But she was already out the door and scurrying into her apartment next door. Sean stood there for a moment and contemplated going after her. They needed to talk. He had a bad feeling about this. Really bad. He'd more than crossed the line with Katie tonight, and he needed to put things back to the way they used to be.

"Sean?"

He hesitated. Then sighing, he shut his door and turned to face the other woman.

By the time he'd sent a not-very-happy Heather on her way thirty minutes later, Katie's apartment was in darkness. From his adjoining deck out back, he stared at her bedroom window, hoping for some sign of movement that would tell him she was awake. There was none. Only darkness and silence.

Driving both hands through his hair, Sean leaned on the rail of the deck and turned away to stare up at the sky. The

moon slid behind a thicket of clouds, taking with it the soft
glow and giving the night a somber feeling. It matched his
mood, Sean decided. The guilt that had hopped onto his
shoulders following that melt-the-fillings-in-his-teeth kiss
with Katie had grown heavier by the minute. Never in a
million years had he intended to complicate things this way.

''Complicate things?'' he muttered. Screwed things up
was more like it. How could he not have, after jumping her
that way? And he had jumped her.

Sean winced at the admission. After all the flack he'd
given Michael about Katie, he had been the one to jump
her. He still couldn't believe he'd done it. He wasn't even
sure how it had happened. One minute she'd been spouting
off something about his unsuitability as a daddy candidate
and the next minute he'd had her in his arms and they were
kissing.

And talk about a kiss! There hadn't been anything the
least bit friendly or brotherly about that kiss. Had it not
been for Heather's untimely arrival, he doubted things
would have stopped at a kiss, either.

He had to make things right with her. Katie and he had
been friends too long, and she was too important to him to
louse things up because his hormones had gone wacko. He
sent another glance toward her dark apartment, and, giving
up, he headed inside. First thing in the morning, Sean promised himself, he'd set things right. He stripped out of his
clothes and slid naked between the sheets. Tucking his
hands behind his head, he lay back on the bed, keenly
aware of the unfulfilled ache below his waist. An ache that,
had he been so inclined, Heather would have been happy
to ease for him.

Man, what a mess. He'd pursued the luscious blonde for
months, and when she finally offered him the heaven he

had been so eager to discover with her in his bed, he'd realized that it wasn't Heather he wanted. It was Katie. And fool or not, he never believed in using a woman that way, so he'd sent Heather home.

As far as exploring that avenue with Katie—no way. She was his friend. Maybe she claimed she didn't want the magic and fairy tales anymore, but he suspected that deep inside, Katie still wanted them. Since he was no fairy-tale prince and didn't possess an ounce of magic in his soul, he would continue to be her friend instead. Just friends.

First thing in the morning he'd hightail it next door to her place and apologize. Then he'd give her his solemn vow that it wouldn't happen again. And as much as he disapproved of her crazy scheme, he'd go ahead and check out her daddy candidates for her.

But thoughts of Katie being pregnant and having a baby did little to relax Sean. "It's going to be a long night," he grumbled and punched at his pillow. Maybe just to make sure his hormones didn't ambush him again, he would give Heather a call in the morning. If he fell in lust with Heather again, it would be easy to get things back to normal between him and Katie.

"And Michael accuses me of not planning," Sean muttered, pleased at his decision. A grin spread across his lips. Tomorrow he'd set everything straight. Everything would work out just the way he planned.

Nothing was working out the way that he had planned, Sean admitted. Frustration gnawed at him. Katie had slipped out of the apartment before he'd awakened, and when he'd gotten home last night, she was already asleep. The fact that his rendezvous with Heather, which was the reason he'd been so late to begin with, had proven a bust for both of them only added to his frustration. But every time he closed his eyes and kissed her, it wasn't Heather's face he saw. It was Katie's, and his conscience wouldn't let him continue.

Not that Heather didn't try to change his mind, Sean admitted. He hated the fact that he'd disappointed her. But he had, and it was all Katie's fault. The woman had him tied up in knots.

Discovering Katie gone before the crack of dawn again this morning had done nothing to improve his mood. Scowling, Sean balled up the sheet of notes he'd written on his pad and pitched it at the trash can across his office. He missed—again.

"You're losing your touch, ace," Michael said from the doorway, looking perfectly polished and pressed as always, which only added to Sean's annoyance. "A two-year-old could do better than that."

"Just let me know when you're ready for some one-on-one, old man, and we'll see who's lost their touch."

"If I wasn't up to my eyeballs with paperwork, I'd take you up on it," Michael told him. Coming into the office, he tossed an envelope marked "Confidential" on Sean's desk.

"Right. Whatever that is I don't want it. You can take it and get out," Sean snapped.

Michael arched his brow. "What's eating at you? Miss Body Beautiful get smart and dump you for someone with more brains?"

"It's not my brains the lady's interested in." Michael was the last person with whom he intended to confess his lapse in character where Katie was concerned. Scooping up the envelope, he opened it, then frowned as he scanned the negative response to his request for verification of an apartment lease on Eric Hartmann, one of Katie's daddy candidates.

"Then what's eating you?" Michael asked.

"Nothing."

"Right. That why you look like you lost your best friend?"

The comment was too close to the mark for comfort. Sean shoved the report back into the envelope and kicked away from his desk. "I had a late night. All right?"

Michael shook his head and gave him a look of disgust. "When are you going to grow up? Don't you think you're getting a little old for this game of musical bed partners? Maybe Katie's got it half-right. Word is she's thinking about settling down and becoming a mother."

He should have known nothing remained a secret in his family. If Katie told her mother as she'd claimed, then her mother had told their mother. "She wants to get pregnant, not married," Sean informed him.

"Well, not the best way to go about it. But my guess is that if Katie does get pregnant, she'll change her mind about getting married."

"Not according to Katie. Says she's giving up on the idea altogether. Kissed too many frogs who didn't turn into a prince."

Michael chuckled. "Yeah. Well, wait and see what happens. All I know is that if I was the guy who got her pregnant, you can bet I'd convince her to marry me."

"Well, you're not going to get her pregnant," Sean informed him heatedly.

"So that's the way it is," Michael said, amusement in his voice.

"You don't know what you're talking about. Katie and I are just friends," Sean informed him.

"Did I say otherwise?" Michael asked innocently.

"Go to hell." Swiping the envelope from his desk, Sean

headed out the door with the sound of Michael's laughter behind him.

"Miss Katie. Miss Katie," little Sarah Evers called to her from the sandbox.

"What is it, sweetie?" Katie asked, stooping down to run a hand over the little blond head.

"Would you help me and Missy build a sand castle?"

"Sure thing," she told them, and settled down to help the two toddlers.

Within thirty minutes, she had another three of the nursery's charges helping them, and was finishing up her own version of Beauty and the Beast, where the princess is the one who saves the prince.

"Tell us another story, Miss Katie," said Spencer, a black-haired toddler with blue eyes that reminded her of Sean.

"Not today, pumpkin. We need to finish this castle."

"How's this, Miss Katie?"

"That's good, Allie. Just make sure you pack the sand around that turret."

She was an expert on castles, having built more than her fair share of the sand kind and the imaginary ones that had white picket fences, a husband and babies. And as far as sand castles went, this one was pitiful, Katie admitted. The clump of wet sand that was supposed to be a tower leaned drunkenly, and the bridge, well the bridge resembled a gopher's tunnel.

"Nick, that moat's deep enough. You dig any deeper and you're going to hit China."

The boy smiled, giving her a gap-toothed grin, that had her heart melting.

"Well, I guess this explains why half of the three-and-four-year-old group haven't come inside for story time,"

Anna O'Neill, the nursery's owner said. She stood with her hands on her hips, a smile on her face, as she looked down at Katie and the assorted little ones working on the castle.

"Guilty as charged," Katie told the older woman who had started the school fifteen years earlier when her own grandchildren were small.

"Miss Katie's helping us build a sand castle," Sarah explained.

"So that's what it is," Anna said softly, an amused look in her eyes.

"You guys finish up," Katie told them, dusting sand from her legs and hands as she stood. "We need to get you cleaned up so you can go listen to Miss Anna's story. I heard she has a new one."

"What is it?"

"Can we have Cinderella?"

Anna chuckled. "Do as Miss Katie says, and you'll see."

"Sorry. I didn't realize I'd kept them out here so long."

Anna tilted her head and studied Katie. "You're the only one of my teachers who ever gets down in that sandbox and plays with them."

Katie shrugged. "I like playing with them. They're neat little people. Besides, I've always been a sucker for sand castles."

"And fairy tales?" Anna asked. "I heard part of that story you were telling them. Quite an interesting twist."

"I wanted to give them something a little different from the ones I grew up with, particularly the girls."

"That's not a bit of cynicism I'm hearing, is it?"

"Maybe just a little."

The children saved her from discussing it further. She accepted sandy hugs and kisses, then sent them in ahead of her to get cleaned up.

"You're really good with them, Katie. It's a shame you

don't have a houseful of your own. I know you've had a few disappointments, but I hope it hasn't soured you on the idea of having a family of your own someday.''

"It hasn't," she said honestly as she walked to the nursery's main building. At least, she wasn't soured on the idea of having children. She wanted to have a baby, a little one to love and call her own. And because she did, she knew she would have to face Sean soon to see what information he'd been able to gather for her on her candidates.

But seeing Sean meant exposing herself to the danger of all those crazy feelings and dreams he managed to stir up inside her. Crazy feelings and dreams like the ones she'd been spinning in her head and heart about Sean loving her, about the two of them getting married, having babies of their own. At least that had been the direction she had been heading in before reality had shown up in the form of Heather Harrison.

Still, the man had a way of making her forget all about common sense. And common sense told her she had better be darn careful because she was on the verge of falling in love with him. But she wasn't in love with him yet, Katie told herself, even when that achy feeling stole into her chest again. She may have made some dumb mistakes in her life, given her heart when she shouldn't have. But loving Sean Fitzpatrick would be the dumbest mistake of all, and it was one mistake she wasn't going to make.

Maybe she had made another mistake, Katie mused, when she spotted Sean seated on the stairs outside of the apartment complex. Just looking at him had her heart beating wildly.

Ditch the fantasies, Katie. Don't you remember what happened the other night?

Oh, she remembered. That was part of the problem. He'd

kissed her senseless, and she wanted to have him do it again. Opening her trunk, Katie removed the bag filled with textbooks for her and storybooks for the children. Still it was hard for a girl not to fantasize a little, she reasoned, as she noted how the moonlight kissed his face, caressed those sharp cheekbones, lingered on that poet's mouth.

She must be a masochist, Katie decided, because her traitorous pulse began to stammer as she locked her car and started toward him. He stood when she approached the stairs. Feet spread apart, arms folded, his mouth frowning. His eyes shifted from a stormy blue to the color of a winter sky, and only then did she realize he was spitting mad. Judging by the way he was glaring at her, Katie surmised that she was the person with whom he was angry.

"Hi," she said, doing her best to manage a friendly smile.

"I didn't realize nursery schools operated until past midnight."

Katie arched a brow at his tone. "They don't." Pushing past him, she started up the stairs.

Sean was on her heels in a heartbeat, looming over her as she entered the hallway leading to her apartment. She shoved her key into the locked door. "Then where in the devil have you been? I was worried sick."

He was worried? "Not that it's any of your business," she managed in an even tone. "But I had a class tonight." Entering the apartment, she flipped on the lights and dropped her bag onto a chair.

"Until midnight?" he demanded, following her inside.

Katie turned around to face him. "What is this? The Grand Inquisition? I had a date after class." And she'd purposefully steered clear of Sean until she'd been sure she had all those feelings for him packed away and firmly under control. But one look at his too handsome face and all her hard work wasn't worth spit. She could feel herself weakening.

"You're right. I was out of line. I'm sorry," he said, regret in his voice. He washed a hand over his face. "I...I really was worried about you, Katie. I was afraid you had an accident, or something had happened to you."

Touched more than she wanted to be, Katie tried to joke. "Hey, fella, I'm a big girl now, remember? Though I appreciate it, you don't need to worry about me. I've been taking care of myself for a long time."

"Yeah, I know. But..." He rubbed a hand at the back of his neck. "Trouble is I do worry about you. You're important to me, Malloy. I don't want anything to happen to you...to us."

"To us?"

"I don't want to lose you or have you upset with me because of...because of my dumb behavior the other night."

"You talking about that silly little kiss?" It was a skinny reference to a kiss that had been a heck of a lot more than that. But she figured the fib was safer for both of them.

He shoved his hands into his pockets. "Yeah. I was way out of line, and I'm sorry. I don't know what got into me, coming on to you like that."

"Sheesh! What's a harmless little kiss between old friends? I can't believe you got yourself all worked up or were worried that I would misunderstand. It was all that wine we drank." At least that's what she had concluded had caused Sean to kiss her as he did in the first place.

"We didn't drink all that much," he asserted.

She shrugged. "Maybe not, but if you toss in a little moonlight. A little chemistry. And I imagine that your ego was a bit dented, too, given the way Heather had been making you chase her. Mix all that up and something's bound to happen. So we shared a kiss. Big deal. I mean, it's not like it's the first time we've ever kissed.'' Of course, she wasn't about to admit that she'd been hearing wedding bells and dreaming of white picket fences.

"Yeah. I seem to recall a game of Spin the Bottle when you were thirteen and wearing braces. You wanted me to teach you to French kiss.''

"Don't remind me,'' Katie said with a groan. "I was in the throes of adolescence and determined to become a woman. I only picked you because Mary Jo Pemberton said you were the best kisser in the tenth grade.''

"Good old Mary Jo.'' He gave her a teasing grin that had those butterflies making a return appearance in her stomach. "I wonder whatever happened to her? She was an excellent student.''

"Excellent student?''

"Yeah. But so were you,'' he said, his eyes shifting to her mouth.

"No thanks to you. You swore you cut your tongue on my braces.''

He wiggled his eyebrows. "Ah, but it was worth it.''

Katie laughed, just as she was meant to do. "That's what he says now,'' she said in a falsetto voice. She should be relieved, she told herself. She didn't want Sean feeling guilty over that steamy kiss. She certainly didn't want him to suspect that she'd been shaken up big-time.

"I must have been one heck of a teacher because you turned out to be a pretty good kisser.''

"Like you deserve the credit?''

"Sure. I'm the guy who taught you how to French kiss, remember?''

She tipped up her chin. "You were only one of many,'' she informed him.

"Brat.'' He snagged her around the waist.

Katie laughed again and flattened her palms against his chest. Suddenly Sean's heartbeat quickened, started to hammer beneath her palm. She glanced up, past the shadow of whiskers dotting his chin to stare into eyes that had darkened like a summer sky. All the teasing and easy banter faded. The fingers at her waist tightened, and for a moment she was positive he was going to kiss her. Instead he released her and stepped back.

Katie dropped her hands, told herself she wasn't disappointed. Plastering a friendly grin on her face, she asked, "So, are we square, Fitzpatrick? Pals, again?"

"Sure. Pals."

"Okay, pal, unless there's something else you needed, you'd better scoot. It's nearly one in the morning."

"I almost forgot. I've started the investigations for you," he said, a frown creasing his brow. "I'm getting responses back on some of my inquiries, and most of them look okay. Except for one I got back today on Eric Hartmann. Some of the data didn't check out. I'm going to need you to fill in a few more blanks for me on him before I can proceed. Do you want to go over this now? Or would you rather wait until morning?"

"Now's okay with me, if it won't take too long."

"Just a couple of minutes to make sure I didn't get my information wrong."

"Fine. Want something to drink? I've got a pitcher of iced tea."

"Tea would be great."

When she returned with the tea, Sean was on the deck. It was a perfect summer night—all soft and warm, with stars sparkling in the sky like diamonds. The gardens beyond the deck bloomed with color—roses in pinks, reds and white, and lilac bushes filled with clusters of purple flowers. Raindrops shimmered like jewels on the green leaves of the shrubbery, and the perfumed scent of lilacs and rain whispered in the breeze. Sean stood on the deck with the moonlight washing over him, looking tall and strong and noble. For a moment, just for a moment, longing seeped through Katie as she watched him, sneaking its way into her heart.

Oh, no you don't, Katie Malloy. She squelched the yearning and stepped outside to join him. "I hope raspberry tea's okay."

"Sure," Sean told her, taking the tray from her and placing it on the table.

She poured them each a glass. "So, what other information do you need on Eric?"

"Just a couple of things," Sean told her. "You said he's a traveling salesman and on the road a lot."

"That's right."

"Does he have a residence besides the one you gave me as his address here in Chicago?"

"Not that I know of. Why?"

"Because a request for verification on his lease came back negative. Could he have a roommate you don't know about whose name the lease would be under?"

"I don't think so. He's never mentioned anyone."

"What about a company-leased apartment?"

"I guess that's possible. He works for a big firm with lots of subsidiaries. He's from Houston originally, and I think that's where he said his company's headquarters are." She sensed something was bothering Sean. "What is it?"

Leaning forward, Sean said, "Honey, you know this guy, and I don't. But I have to tell you, I don't like the feel of this. My gut tells me he's bad news."

"You don't know that."

"You're right. I don't. But I don't want to see you get hurt again. I just want you to be happy."

"I will be. Just help me find the right man to father my baby."

"Will a baby really be enough, Katie?"

"For me it will. It will be more than I've ever had before."

Four

The guy was married!

Sean stared at the documents spread out across his desk. Fury rose in his throat, nearly choking him, as he studied the copy of the marriage certificate. It only verified what he'd known in his gut for the past week. Katie's number-one daddy candidate, Eric Alan Hartmann, the fellow she'd been out with for three nights this week already, was a married man. The jerk and his unfortunate wife would be celebrating their sixth wedding anniversary in two months.

His gaze shifted to the photostat of the other incriminating documents he'd received. Birth certificates—one dated three years ago and another fourteen months ago—for Ashley and Alan Hartmann. The no-good louse was not only married, but he already had two kids.

But the real prize, Sean decided, picking up the final thing that put murder in his heart and blood in his eye, was the medical record on Hartmann that he'd managed to get his hands on. The dirty snake had had a vasectomy a year ago—just after the birth of his son. Sean crushed the paper in his fist.

No wonder he'd told Katie that he loved kids and wanted to be a father. The creep already *was* a father—*and* a husband. And he knew he could take Katie to bed without a single worry that she would actually get pregnant.

He was going to kill the SOB. But first…first, he had to break the news to Katie.

Sean was still trying to break the news to Katie later that evening when he'd shown up at the coffeehouse and carried a cup over to the table where she and Hartmann sat.

"What a surprise running into you here," Katie said, her whisky-colored eyes studying him suspiciously over the rim of her cup of cappuccino.

"I finished an appointment nearby and decided to grab a cup of coffee before heading home." Of course he'd known Katie and Hartmann had theater tickets for tonight. She'd mentioned it to him—in one of those rare moments when she'd actually been home—in response to his suggestion that they grab a pizza together tonight. He'd also known from experience that after the performance, Katie would insist on going down the street to the coffeehouse. There was something to be said for knowing someone so well, Sean thought. He just wished he had been able to see her alone for a moment and break the news about Hartmann to her in private.

Anger churned in his blood as he glared at Hartmann. He wanted to knock the guy's lights out. But first he had to tell Katie. And how was he supposed to do that when she was looking at the man with stars in her eyes?

The man was all surface, Sean deduced, noting the neat, perfectly styled blond hair, the odd-shade-of-green eyes. He'd bet his favorite basketball jersey that that shade of green came from tinted contact lenses. Even the guy's tan looked perfect. Too perfect. Probably came from a bottle, Sean mused. The fact that Hartmann was wearing a suit and hadn't so much as loosened his tie was one more thing to dislike about the guy. He looked like an advertisement for *GQ*.

Unlike him. Sean glanced down at his own attire of faded jeans and the denim shirt rolled up to his elbows. He looked at his own hands, darkened by the sun, scarred and callused from work and play. He didn't need a mirror to know that his hair was anything but neat. He'd ridden with the window down on his Bronco, and he hadn't taken time to go in for a trim in more than two months. Uncertainty inched its way up Sean's spine. What did Katie see when she looked at him? Did she compare him to Hartmann? Did he fall short in her eyes?

"Kind of late for an appointment, isn't it?" Katie asked him pointedly.

"Not at all," Sean told her, absconding with half of her chocolate biscotti. "With my job, you can't count on working bankers' hours."

"Just what kind of work is it you do?" Eric asked, before flashing another of those poster-boy smiles.

"I'm a PI—private investigator." Sean dipped the biscotti in his coffee. "I dig up dirt on people," he added.

"You sound like a character out of an old Raymond Chandler novel," Katie accused. "Sean and his brothers have a private investigation agency."

The dimples in Mr. Too-Good-to-Be-True's pretty face dimmed. "Must be interesting work. What kind of...uh, investigating is it that you do exactly?"

Sean leaned back in his seat and smiled. "Oh, a little of this. A little of that." He took his time, giving Hartmann time to chew on the possibilities. He wanted the worm to squirm before he crushed him. It gnawed at him something fierce, every time he thought of the game Hartmann had been playing with Katie and how close Katie had been to asking the man to get her pregnant. He was going to make sure Hartmann not only sweated, but that he hurt, too. But he had to figure out a way to do it without causing Katie too much pain.

"Don't you, Sean?"

Sean jerked his attention back to Katie. "Sorry, what was that?"

"I was telling Eric that you do a lot of insurance fraud investigations. Isn't that right?"

"Some. I also do employment verifications, missing persons, divorces, cheating spouses. And personal background searches—which is where digging up the dirt on people comes in. If someone's hiding something…say, a marriage, or kids…you can bet I'll find out about it."

The man's face went white beneath his tan. Sean gave him a wide grin.

"Eric just received another promotion," Katie said, shooting Sean another menacing look as she attempted to change the direction of conversation. She shifted her focus to Hartmann, and her eyes sparkled as they came to rest on the other man. "Eric's been appointed as the regional manager for his firm."

"Congratulations," Sean said dryly.

"Thanks. Unfortunately, the promotion means that I'm going be on the road even more than I am now."

That's right, worm, Sean thought. Weasel your way out of this. You know I'm on to you and am about to blow your little scam.

"Which means I won't get to see Katie as much as I'd liked to." He kissed the tips of Katie's fingers and gazed lovingly into her eyes. "Makes me almost wonder if I should just turn down the company's offer."

"Don't even think such a thing," Katie said, but her face glowed at the compliment.

Sean thought he was going to be sick. Since he couldn't very well punch out the guy without first explaining to Katie his reasons, he considered dumping a glass of ice water over pretty boy's head to take some of the steam out of the way Hartmann was devouring Katie with his eyes. He didn't like that hungry look on the man's face. Not one bit.

But he could hardly blame the guy, Sean admitted, as he slanted a glance at Katie. That little black number with the shoestring straps she was wearing certainly made the most of her long legs, and it didn't do a thing to hide her curves. Skinny or not, she looked great—a fact that the male in him was finding difficult to ignore.

Katie laughed at something the other man whispered to her. Circling the rim of the water glass with an itchy finger, Sean glared at Hartmann. "I suppose a guy who's on the road as much as you are, is sort of like a sailor. You know, always shipping in and out of different ports. Must meet a lot of women that way."

Still holding Katie's hand, Hartmann shifted his attention to Sean. His perfectly white teeth gleamed in his tanned face, and silently Sean promised himself the fellow would be making a trip to the dentist. "Yeah, I guess I do meet a lot of women. There are certainly plenty of females in the medical field today, and everyone, male and female alike, is eager to learn all they can about the high-tech medical equipment my company sells. But it can get pretty lonely being on the road so much. But then it makes me look forward to coming home because I know that I'll get to see Katie again."

"What a sweet thing to say," Katie gushed.

"It's true," Eric told her. "I do look forward to being with you."

"How do you feel about Katie's plans to get pregnant?"

"Sean, really—"

"Let him answer, Katie," he told her, knowing from the look on her face that she was going to make him pay for this later.

As though sensing his hostility, the other man shifted uncomfortably in his seat. "Actually I was surprised when Katie first told me about her idea. Flattered, of course, that she would consider asking me to be the father of her child. But I did have some reservations."

"And now?" Sean prompted.

Hartmann cleared his throat. "Well, as I told Katie, I like children, but working and traveling like I do makes it difficult to find time for a relationship that would lead to a family."

"So you're willing to go along with Katie's plan and try to get her pregnant?"

"Absolutely," he said, a man-to-man smile on his lips.

Sean gritted his teeth. "So you don't have a problem with getting a woman pregnant and leaving her to raise your child alone?"

"Sean—"

"It's all right, Katie." Eric patted her hand. "It's obvious Sean cares about you and is concerned. To answer your question, yes, I would have a problem getting a woman pregnant and leaving her to raise my child alone. But as Katie's explained it to me, she and I would share in the parental responsibilities, so she wouldn't be left alone."

Violence stirred in Sean's blood. He tightened his fingers around the coffee mug, wishing that it was Hartmann's throat. "Would you marry Katie if you got her pregnant?"

"That's enough, Sean!"

He ignored Katie's warning, and the heads twisting in their direction from nearby tables. "Would you marry her?" he demanded, his voice little more than a growl.

A bead of perspiration trickled down the other man's temples. His Adam's apple worked up and down beneath the silk tie. "I think marriage is something that Katie and I would both have to discuss. But put your mind at ease, Sean. I do care for Katie and if we made a baby together, I would do my best to persuade her to marry me."

"But that's not going to happen, is it, Hartmann?" Sean came to his feet and came around the table. He grabbed Hartmann by his shirtfront and yanked him to his feet. "You know there's no chance you'll ever marry her because you know you can't get her pregnant." Baring his teeth, Sean curled his fist, tightening it in the man's shirt collar and said, "But you're more than willing to lie to Katie so you can take her to bed, aren't you?"

"I don't know what you're talking about." Hartmann protested. He struggled to free himself from Sean's grip.

"How about your vasectomy? And, of course, there's the little matter of your—"

"That's enough!"

Sean heard the chair scraping on the tile floor, and out of the corner of his eye, he could see more heads angling in their direction.

Then Katie filled his line of vision as she pushed her way between the two of them, forcing him to release his hold on Hartmann. Angry color climbed up her cheeks. Temper darkened her eyes, making them shine like polished amber.

Katie angled her angry gaze in Eric's direction. "I don't know if what Sean said is true—"

"It's true." Sean closed his mouth when she fired another furious look at him.

"Whether it's true or not, I hope you don't think for one moment that I would have been foolish enough to sleep with you for the sole purpose of getting pregnant without first insisting on a sperm count test."

Sean nearly choked. It had never occurred to him that Katie would think to require such a thing. Probably because he hadn't thought of it. From Hartmann's expression, neither had he.

"And for the record, I want a baby not a husband. I have no intention of marrying you or anyone else."

The snicker died on Sean's lips when she turned and slapped those stormy eyes on him. "As for you," she said, a scowl lining her face. "When I want your opinions about how to run my life, I'll ask for them. Until then, butt out."

"Katie," Eric began, "the things Fitzpatrick told you—"

"I think," she said, enunciating each word. "That I've been embarrassed enough for one night. I'd like to go home. Now."

Sean had never seen Katie so angry. She snatched up her purse and the lacy shawl thing from a chair and headed for the exit without giving either Hartmann or him a backward glance.

Hartmann practically tripped over himself running after her. Tossing some bills on the table, Sean followed them to the parking lot at a quickened pace. No way was Hartmann going to take Katie home, he decided. He spied Katie standing next to the sleek-looking red sports car, tapping her foot impatiently.

Hartmann was fumbling with the door lock when Sean

reached them. He clamped a fist around Katie's arm. "Shove off, Hartmann. I'll see that she gets home."

The other man's head jerked up. His mouth thinned. "In case you didn't notice, Katie's with me."

"Not anymore, she isn't. Come on, Katie."

Katie jerked free. "What's gotten into you?"

"You don't want to be with this guy. He's—"

"He's my date, and we obviously have a few things to discuss." Turning away from Sean, she started toward the Porsche.

"Wrong," Sean told her before snagging her by the waist and swinging her up over his shoulder.

"What do you think you're doing?"

He headed across the parking lot. "Taking you home."

"Now hang on a minute, Fitzpatrick," Hartmann called out as he chased behind them. "You heard Katie. She and I have a lot to talk about."

"Send her a letter," Sean tossed back.

"Put me down this instant!"

"Whatever you say." Pulling open the door of his Bronco, he dumped her onto the passenger seat. If looks could kill, he would die right there on the spot, Sean thought, before slamming the door shut.

Hartmann blocked his path. "Where do you get off pulling this stunt? You can't stop me from seeing Katie."

"Want to bet?" Sean countered, before planting his fist in the other man's face.

Katie squealed and scrambled from the truck. She grabbed Sean's arm when he would have gone after him again. "Don't!"

"You're crazy," Hartmann accused. "I think you broke my jaw."

Sean stood over the fallen man, placed his foot on his

chest. "You ever come near Katie again, and I'll break every bone in your body."

The moment Sean pulled the Bronco up alongside the curb, Katie jumped out, not even bothering to wait for him to bring the truck to a complete stop.

"Are you crazy?" he yelled after her.

Probably, she wanted to scream as she slammed the door shut. But she refused to waste her breath. She was crazy all right—crazy for believing Sean would help her. Instead he'd humiliated her, behaved like a testosterone-laden male, and he'd broken poor Eric's jaw. Cursing the high-heeled pumps and the narrow cut of her dress that hampered her stride, Katie fumed as she stormed down the sidewalk toward the apartment complex.

The truck door slammed behind her. "Katie! Would you wait a damn minute?"

Not bothering to acknowledge him, she hiked the dress up to the tops of her hose and hastened up the stairs of the complex. Fury made her fingers shake as she jammed her key into the lock. The nerve of him, treating her as if she were a…a child. And he called himself her friend?

"Ha! Some friend he turned out to be." Footsteps sounded on the stairs behind her when, finally, the lock clicked. Katie zipped inside her apartment just as Sean reached her door.

"Katie—"

She slammed the door in his face and felt a small measure of satisfaction at the yelp which followed. Serves you right.

"Damn it, Katie." A fist pummeled the door. "Open the door. I have to talk to you."

"The time to talk to me was before you decided to make me the laughingstock of the coffeehouse tonight."

"That's what I need to explain," he said, exasperation in his voice. "I—"

"I'm not interested in your explanations, Fitzpatrick, and I don't want to see you." She flipped off the outside lights.

His fists hit the door again. "Dammit, Katie!"

Ignoring him, Katie turned on her heel and started for her bedroom. Anger clung to her, and was still pumping through her system fast and furious when she stepped into her bedroom. She stood on the thick plush carpet, amid the familiar splashes of teal and rose and lemon. There was nothing drab or dull about her bedroom. It was a riot of color and scents. And it never failed to cheer her. Until now. Instead images of the horrible scene with Sean and Eric played over and over in her head.

She had never been so embarrassed in her life! Why hadn't Sean just told her about the vasectomy instead of springing it on her the way he had?

"Because he's a jerk. That's why. A macho jerk." She tossed her evening bag on the four-poster bed. Her shawl followed. Then she kicked off the ridiculous high-heeled shoes, sending them clear across the room.

Temper seething inside her, Katie yanked down the zipper of her dress. It stalled midway down her back. She pulled harder, heaping a plague of misfortunes on the head of the dress's designer.

If she lived to be a hundred, she would never understand the male of the species. And the man she understood least of all was Sean Fitzpatrick. The man made her crazy, which was nothing new. He'd been driving her batty since they were kids. But tonight... She sucked in a breath and tried rezipping the dress and starting over. Tonight Sean had gone too far. Whether he approved of her plan or not, he'd had no right to interfere as he had, and to treat her like...like some helpless twit. Just thinking of how he'd behaved—charging in like some kind of Sir Galahad, decking Eric and tossing her over his shoulder—made her want to scream. He'd been out of line—way out of line. He wasn't her brother, and he certainly wasn't her lover. Okay, so she *had* asked him to check the guys out. But to interrupt her date?

Now be honest, Katie girl. Were you really having that great a time with Eric?

Oh, how she hated that pesky voice of her conscience. All right, so things hadn't been all that exciting, she admitted. Maybe she had grown a tad tired of listening to Eric talk about his big promotion and how much money he was going to make. She tried easing the zipper down gently this time. The blasted thing stalled again in the same spot.

And the chemistry?

Okay, so there weren't any sparks between her and Eric. What little chemistry had once existed just sort of fizzled out sometime around their third date. So what? Until Sean had dropped that bomb about the vasectomy, Eric had been the perfect choice. The man was bright, educated, responsible and handsome to boot. He liked kids, and he had been receptive to her proposition about a baby.

And he was as dull as dishwater. If she was going to be forced to tell the truth at least to herself, she had been bored silly tonight—at least until Sean had shown up.

Katie scowled. That still didn't let Sean off the hook. He'd had no right to act like some overzealous, outraged Sir Galahad hell-bent on protecting her virtue. Growing irritated all over again, as much with the dress as with Sean, she gave the zipper another yank.

Nothing.

Her virtue didn't need protecting. She didn't need a Sir Galahad. And she certainly didn't need Sean Fitzpatrick acting like some kind of…some kind of jealous lover.

A shudder rippled through her at the thought of Sean as her lover, and for a moment she abandoned her battle with the zipper. Just because they had shared a few kisses didn't mean anything. They were friends, good friends. Nothing more. Hadn't she been over this in her head a hundred times during the past few weeks?

Sean wasn't interested in anything more than friendship from her—which was fine because she felt the same way.

Are you sure, Katie?

Her stomach tightened like an invisible fist, and Katie decided she really didn't like her busybody conscience one bit. A shiver whispered down her spine at the memory of that steamy kiss the night of her birthday dinner. No one had ever kissed her in quite that way before—hungrily, possessively. She wasn't going to let herself fall in love with him. Absolutely not.

Katie gave the zipper another determined tug as though freeing herself from the dress would somehow free her from her thoughts about Sean. When the metal tongue slid the rest of the way down the track, she breathed a sigh of relief. Shimmying out of the dress, she let it fall to the floor around her ankles.

"Dammit, Katie. You nearly broke my nose," Sean accused as he came barreling into her bedroom and came to a dead stop.

Five

Sean froze, unable to breathe at the sight of Katie wearing tiny black panties, sheer stockings and nothing else. Moonlight spilled through the window, illuminating her like a spotlight. Her body had gone statue still, not a single muscle moved—except for her eyes. The dark fire that snapped in those brown eyes, slowly gave way to a new kind of heat, a heat that mirrored the one that had been raging in his bloodstream from the first moment he'd seen her tonight wearing that excuse for a dress. Only now she wasn't wearing the dress. Unable to stop himself, Sean slid his gaze down her slim torso. He imagined peeling away the hands covering her breasts and replacing them with his own. He flexed his fingers, and could almost feel her silky, soft flesh as he stroked and shaped each curve, each limb, each inch of her body.

Desire whipped through him faster than sound, hitting

him with the force of a knockout punch and evoking a wild, frantic beat in his heart. He wanted to touch her, to memorize her with his fingers, with his mouth, the same way he was touching and memorizing her with his eyes. He took a step toward her.

"Sean!"

His name was a hiss on her lips that slapped down his fantasies. Dragging in several deep breaths, Sean struggled to free himself from the grips of this mad desire that had nearly driven him to do something crazy.

"W-what are you doing here?" she demanded as she scrambled to retrieve the skinny black dress lying at her feet. She snatched up the thing and held it in front of her like a shield. "And how...how did you get in?"

Tearing his gaze away from the tempting picture she made, Sean forced himself to focus on the plant over her shoulder near the window. "I used the key you gave me," he finally managed, swallowing past the huge lump lodged in his throat. "Remember, we exchanged keys a long time ago." And while Katie had used her key to his place often in order to care for his plants and mail when he was away, he'd never had occasion or the need to use the one she'd given him. Until tonight. Tonight he'd been desperate.

"Well, you shouldn't have come here. Haven't you already done enough?"

He winced at the accusation. It was true, he had handled things badly. That's why he had to explain. "I...we need to talk."

"I told you, I don't want to talk anymore tonight. I want you to go, Sean. Now. We-we'll talk later."

"Later isn't good enough. We need to talk now." His eyes wandered back to her, and all his good intentions turned to mush. Desire slammed through him again. She stood nearly naked before him, with her face flushed, her skin looking whisper soft and her eyes shimmering with nerves and heat. "It can't wait."

The hand clutching the dress to her trembled. "All right. But for pity's sake, wait in the other room while I get dressed."

"Right," he said, jerking his gaze away. "I'll wait in the den." And maybe while he was there, Sean chided, he could get his blasted hormones under control and figure out just what in the hell was the matter with him, ogling and lusting after Katie the way he'd been doing.

Five minutes later he had regained his perspective and some measure of control. Standing in front of the window that led to the deck, he stared out into the moonless night at the storm clouds chasing across the skyline. He still had no neat answers to explain the confounded chemistry that seemed to keep springing full-blown between him and Katie.

"All right. What's so important that couldn't wait?"

Sean applied the brakes on his less-than-sterling thoughts. "I— Would you mind sitting down?" he asked, deciding that Katie seated would be less of a distraction. Noting her hesitation, he added, "Please."

Katie took a seat on the ancient couch that they had found at a garage sale, and that she'd claimed was an antique. Her expression was wary, her chin tipped militantly. "All right. I'm sitting."

Sean took the chair across from her. Leaning forward, he planted his elbows on his knees and met her cool gaze. "First of all, I want to apologize for my behavior tonight."

When she didn't respond, merely crossed her arms and continued to look at him, he expelled a deep breath. "Seems like lately all I do is apologize to you for one thing or another. I guess you're getting pretty tired of hearing me say I'm sorry, huh?''

"Yes, I am. Do you really think saying you're sorry makes up for the way you behaved tonight? You embarrassed me, Sean. You humiliated me in front of a room filled with people, and in front of a man that I care for."

Her words hit him like a slap. "Embarrassing you was never my intention."

"It still doesn't change the fact that you did embarrass me. Why on earth did you pick the coffeehouse to tell me about Eric's vasectomy?"

"Because I didn't have much choice." At her skeptical look, he continued, "I wasn't sure how serious things had gotten between you and Hartmann. You'd been out with the man for three nights running and were making noises about asking him to get you pregnant—in spite of the fact that I told you to wait until I'd finished my investigation of him."

Katie shrugged. "I didn't want to wait. Besides you seemed to be dragging your feet."

"I was trying to be thorough."

She shifted in her seat. "You said nothing negative had come back on Eric. No outstanding traffic tickets or arrest warrants. No bad credit reports, and his apartment was leased by his firm. I'll admit, I didn't know about the vasectomy. But you should have told me in private."

"I didn't find out about it until this afternoon, and you were already off with Romeo." He didn't bother telling her about the phony call he'd made to Hartmann's wife, pretending to do a survey about planned pregnancies among young couples. Luck had been on his side when Elizabeth Hartmann told him that she and her husband had decided two children were enough and had taken measures to ensure

the family didn't expand further. Obtaining the birth certificates and medical records to corroborate his findings had
followed. "Listen, it's not going to do either one of us any
good to debate whether I should or shouldn't have con-
fronted Hartmann. The fact is I did confront him, and I'd
do it again if it meant saving you from doing something
you would regret later."

"Maybe I wouldn't have regretted it."

"For God's sake, Katie, the guy's married!"

Her face paled. "Married?"

"Yes." Cursing his temper, Sean went to her. He knelt
down in front of her, caught her hands in his. Tightening
his fingers over hers, he said, "He's got a wife and two
kids living in Houston."

"Oh, my God!"

He watched as the shock sank in.

"What a fool I was not to see it." She tugged her hands
free and used them to cover her face.

Moving to the couch beside her, Sean pried her fingers
away from her face. He caught her chin in his hands and
stared into those sad brown eyes, vowing that if he ever
ran into Hartmann again, the guy was dead meat. "Listen
to me," he ordered. "You were not a fool. Hartmann was
just very clever. He deceived you."

Katie shook her head. "No. I should have seen it. It was
right there in front of me. All of the business trips, his never
being here on weekends or holidays. Our dates were always
on weeknights. Only an idiot or a fool wouldn't have put
two and two together and come up with four. I should have
realized something was fishy."

"Hard to do when the barracuda's masquerading as a
goldfish."

She gave him a weak smile. "Thanks, but that doesn't excuse my own gullibility."

"Don't be so hard on yourself, Malloy. It could have been worse. Suppose you had slept with the jerk and then found out he had a family?"

"You're right." Katie shuddered. "His poor wife. When I think how close I came to..." She never completed the thought, simply stared down at her hands.

A fist seemed to close around Sean's heart, at the thick sound of tears in Katie's voice. "But you didn't," he said, drawing her into his arms. "The important thing is that you didn't do anything to be ashamed of." He stroked her back, pressed a kiss to her hair.

"Thanks to you," she whispered.

She nuzzled closer, rested her palms against his chest. Her touch set off another land mine of need inside him. The ache below his belt grew more painful by the second, but Sean continued to stroke her back gently, press kisses to her hair, while he fought his own despicable urge to touch her, to taste her.

When her shoulders began to shake, the soft rumble vibrating through her to him, Sean tightened his arms around her. "It's okay, honey. It's okay."

Katie shook her head, but continued to make low, muffled sounds that caused her body to quiver. His heart kicked. Unable to bear seeing her hurt this way, Sean continued to offer comforting words while he pressed more soft kisses against her head, her hair. Tucking her hair behind one ear, he kissed the shell of her ear, the side of her face, her cheek.

By the time he realized that Katie was no longer crying, that the trembling sobs had stopped, her hands had maneuvered from his chest to the back of his head, where her fingers combed through the hair at his neck and stirred up the fires he'd been trying so hard to keep banked. "Better?" he whispered.

She nodded her head.

"Good. If I didn't break that weasel's jaw, I'm going to for breaking your heart like this."

Katie's fingers stilled a moment. "Sean?"

"Hmm?"

"Eric didn't break my heart."

"It's okay, honey. You don't have to lie to me," he said, still hugging her close. "And you don't have to hide your tears from me, either."

She eased back a fraction and looked at him out of eyes that had gone all liquid and warm. "I'm not lying," she said. "And I wasn't crying. I was laughing."

"Laughing?"

"Uh-huh. While I thought Eric was a nice guy, he was about as much fun as a funeral. For the past few days I've been trying to work up some enthusiasm to go to bed with him so I could get pregnant."

Not sure if that news made him happy or feel like a jerk, he said, "I thought you were in love with the guy!"

"In love with him? Where on earth did you get that idea?"

"Where do you think I got it from? From you," he retorted. "You haven't had a moment to spare for me in over a week, and every time I did manage to catch a glimpse of you, all you've done is talk about Hartmann."

"I didn't realize you missed me," she said with a grin.

He glared at her. But he had missed her, Sean admitted. And he had never been a man to pine after a woman before, yet that's exactly what he'd been doing—pining after Katie. Well, it was going to stop. Right now. Katie Malloy had been pushing his buttons for years, he told himself, his temper simmering. And lately she'd begun pushing a whole new set of buttons—dangerous buttons that plugged right into her being a woman and him being a man.

Her eyes sparkling with mischief, she slanted him a glance. "Oh, this is rich," she said, and burst into laughter.

Her laughter pushed Sean over the edge. To hell with it, he decided. Hauling Katie into his arms, he slammed his mouth down on hers. Her throaty laughter melted beneath his lips and emerged as a soft sigh. He kissed her hard, thrusting his tongue in to taste and explore her as he had wanted to do all evening. Desire and an aching tenderness flooded through him. He lifted his head a fraction, and when she didn't take a swing at him, he swooped back down for another taste.

Her mouth yielded easily this time, as though they were lovers already. When she groaned, those dangerous land mines of need that he'd been trying to avoid exploded inside him. He was nuts, Sean told himself. This was Katie. His friend, his pal. But his body didn't seem to be listening, because he deepened the kiss that had already gone way, way too deep. Releasing her mouth, his lips journeyed to her jaw, to her neck, to her collarbone. The taste of her, the smell of her skin, set off another round of explosions.

He stared into her eyes. There was no laughter now. There was no teasing devil in those eyes either. There was only an answering hunger, an answering need. Instead of shoving him away, Katie curled her fists into his shirt and dragged his mouth back to hers. He'd have sworn on his life that he never meant to do more than kiss her. He was thirty-two years old, not some randy teenager who didn't know how to stop a kiss from going too far. But darn if his hands didn't streak over her, down her ribs, the dip in her waist, the rounded curve of her slim hips. And then his fingers sneaked beneath her shirt. She arched her back, filling his palms with her small, firm breasts. Still kissing her, Sean tumbled her back onto the cushions.

He heard a snap. His lust-fogged brain registered that something was wrong, just before a leg of the couch collapsed, dropping them both to the floor and sending lips and teeth clashing together.

Katie yelped.

So did he.

Sitting on the floor beside the crippled couch, Sean sucked in air. He tasted blood in his mouth. Probing his lip with his tongue, he realized it was his. "You all right?" he asked.

"Yes. No." She took another gulp of air, and the glazed expression in her eyes began to clear. She slanted a glance to the lopsided couch. "I knew I should have used something stronger than glue to fix that leg," she said, making a pitiful attempt to joke.

"I'll fix it for you."

He didn't know if it was his offer to fix the blasted couch or something she saw in his face, but suddenly Katie had the look of a rabbit trying to outrun a fox. "Don't worry about it. You have enough to keep you busy. I can take care of it," she said, scrambling to her feet. She paused in the act of straightening her clothes. "You okay?"

Frowning, Sean shoved to his feet. "I'm fine. Katie—"

"You sure? I mean, I don't want you suing me because my couch gave you whiplash."

Sean caught her hands between his. Finally, when she stopped fidgeting, he said, "Tell me what's wrong."

She opened her mouth, closed it, then sighed. "You do

know this is crazy, don't you? Of course you know it. Just like I know it. No way do we want to let a little chemistry get in the way and mess up our friendship now, do we? Of course we don't,'' she replied, not giving him a chance to answer.

She continued to chatter at warp speed. ''So I think the best thing for us both to do is to just forget this happened. I mean, not that anything really happened. Because nothing did happen.'' She glanced at the watch on his wrist. ''Oh, Lord, is that the right time? Is it already after midnight?''

''Yes, but—''

''Sheesh! And both of us have to be at work in the morning. We'd better go to bed...I mean to sleep...I mean to sleep in our own beds...alone...without each other.'' Pulling her hands free, she started toward the door, obviously expecting him to follow. And because she appeared so genuinely distressed, he did.

''Katie, honey—''

''Thanks for everything, Sean. You really are the absolute best friend a girl could have.'' Before he could protest, she gave him a hit-and-run smack to his tender mouth, then shoved him out of the door.

Short of slitting her throat, she didn't see any way for her to get out of going to the Fitzpatricks' annual summer barbecue. Sighing, Katie dragged out her favorite cutoffs and sweatshirt. She may have managed to successfully dodge Sean for the past ten days—thanks in part to a three-day assignment he'd had out of town, a couple of dates and the all-night movie theater across town—but she'd run out of time and excuses. He was back. She'd heard him return late last night, and there was no question that he would be at his family's home for today's festivities.

She pulled the sweatshirt over her head. She wasn't a coward, Katie told herself, but every time she thought of facing Sean after the way she'd practically jumped him on her couch, she got a knot the size of a fist in her stomach. "He probably thinks I'm another sex-starved female," she murmured, and cringed at the thought. Sitting on her bed, Katie slipped on white socks, then buried her face in her hands. She'd rather have a root canal than face Sean.

Lifting her head, she went to her closet and dug out her sneakers. Maybe it wasn't too late to accept Scott's offer to take her dancing or call Paulo and ask him to meet her for coffee. After all, she reasoned, the two were her remaining daddy candidates. Just as quickly, she nixed the idea. After her disaster in judgment where Eric was concerned, she'd promised herself to take things slower with both men until Sean had completed his investigations. Besides, it was becoming harder and harder for her to think of either man as the father of her child. Not because of anything they had done or said, but simply because every time she thought of having a baby now, it was Sean she kept seeing as the father.

Not an option, Katie girl.

Which left the movie theater. Katie wrinkled her nose. She simply couldn't face that dingy little place again. Besides, she'd already seen every movie on the playbill at least twice.

"Face it, kiddo. You've got to see Sean sooner or later." So she might as well get it over with today. Anyway, what choice did she have? Based on the messages left on her answering machine by both Mrs. Fitzpatrick and Molly, even thinking about not showing up for the barbecue would not go down easily. Thoughts of the get-together that packed the Fitzpatricks' backyard with family, friends and neighbors brought a smile to Katie's lips.

Some of her best memories growing up had been from that summer barbecue. For an only child who'd grown up without a father, had lost a stepfather and the various other men who couldn't quite stay with her and her mother, the Fitzpatrick gathering proved to be one of those rare times when Katie almost felt like part of a big family. She'd always looked forward to the event. The fact that she hadn't missed one of the barbecues in the twenty years she'd known the Fitzpatricks—even long after she had moved away—meant that calling today to say she was sick wasn't an option. If she did, Molly and half the Fitzpatricks would be over here in a heartbeat cramming heaven knows what types of Italian and Irish remedies down her throat to make her well.

Katie shuddered at the thought. "Maybe slitting my throat isn't such a bad alternative after all," she muttered as she tied the laces of her sneakers and stood. No. She had to go. And somehow she would have to get through the day without Sean realizing just how badly she'd been shaken by those kisses they had shared.

Shaken? Ha! Try unglued.

Katie snatched her brush from the dresser and, flipping her hair forward, she tamed and secured it with a ponytail tie. She paused, her thoughts once more on Sean. A few kisses, a tender look, and he had managed to sneak his way into her heart. Only this time it wasn't an adolescent crush, and it certainly wasn't friendship. She was in deep, deep trouble, Katie admitted. Despite all her vows to swear off romance, all those lectures to herself and just plain, common sense, Sean had somehow slipped right in and planted himself square in the middle of her heart.

The darned man. No matter what she tried, he flat-out refused to turn into a frog. And every time he kissed her, she kept hearing wedding bells, seeing babies that looked like him and dreaming about fairy-tale endings.

Well, she cared about the man way too much to saddle him with her unwanted feelings and the guilt he'd heap on himself for rejecting her. Because he would reject her. She didn't doubt that for a moment. She wasn't Sean's type. She never had been. Never would be, and he was about as likely to fall in love with her as it was for Chicago to get snow in July. And her sense of self-preservation told her that having Sean walk away from her would be the one rejection she might never be able to get over.

Tossing a bottle of sunscreen in her bag, she snagged her keys and headed out the door. That meant she had to concentrate on being Sean's friend—and stop wishing she was his lover. And if that meant knocking the prince off of his horse, then so help her, she'd send him toppling on his backside if it killed her.

Knocking Sean off that horse wasn't proving to be an easy task, Katie realized two hours later, as she nursed a glass of lemonade and watched him toss a football with his two brothers. Any one of the Fitzpatrick men could make a gal's head spin. After all, few women were immune to the basic package of hard muscles, dark hair, sexy blue eyes and a wicked grin. But putting all three of them together was downright criminal. And for her the most lethal of the three was Sean. He wasn't dressed in anything special— just an old Chicago P.D. T-shirt and gym trunks. But watching those muscles flex and ripple, the legs pump and stretch, the light sheen of sweat turning his skin to a deeper bronze did nothing to calm her pulse.

"Sean! Sean! Want horsey ride!" One of his young cousins streaked across the yard toward him and launched herself at his legs. Laughing, he immediately ditched the football and dropped down to scoop the little girl up into his arms. Within moments, the little heartbreaker was seated on his shoulders and grinning from ear to ear. Katie's heart executed another of those fast tap-dancing numbers. As if she needed help. Her traitorous heart had already been trying to convince her that Sean arriving solo meant that he was no longer smitten with Heather. And maybe, just maybe, that she'd been right in thinking that he couldn't kiss her the way he had, touch her with such aching tenderness and need, and not feel something for her besides friendship.

He galloped around in another circle, then collapsed on the grass with the little imp landing on his chest. When he sat up, he slanted a glance in her vicinity, and Katie's pulse started to stutter. She grabbed her lemonade, took another sip and turned away.

"Safe at last," Molly proclaimed as she dropped down onto the bench across from Katie. Tall and slender with short dark hair and those Fitzpatrick blue eyes, her oldest and dearest friend looked more like a model than a police officer. "Whew! You should have reminded me what a meddling family I have."

Katie chuckled. "You needed a reminder?"

Laughing, she said, "You'd think I'd know better, wouldn't you?"

"One would think so," Katie replied with a smile. Since Molly had moved to Chicago from California a year ago, the family had formed a protective pack around their cousin. Not for the first time, Katie wished her own family had shared that type of closeness. "What's up?" she asked her friend.

"Evidently Uncle Keegan's been talking to my dad. I just got a thorough grilling about the dangers of a female trying to do a man's job."

"I can imagine." A retired police officer, Sean's father was clearly into traditional roles—as were most of the Fitzpatrick men. "He'd better not let your aunt hear him."

"She did," Molly informed her with a grin. "Told him she had a real man's job for him to do. Then she handed him a tray of hamburger patties and pointed him toward the grill."

"A woman after my own heart," Katie said with affection as she thought of Sean's mother. "You've got to admire her. Not many women could hold her own in a houseful of men the way she has. I imagine between Mr. F. and her four sons, she had her work cut out for her."

"You're probably right. But I pity my cousins. The woman is seriously into becoming a grandmother, now that Ryan's wife is expecting. According to her, all of her boys should be married and providing her with the grandchildren she thinks she deserves. She's not at all happy that Michael and Sean have both passed the ancient age of thirty and are still single."

Katie chuckled. "Must be something in the iced tea they're drinking, because I got a similar song from my mother not five minutes after I got here. How did you manage to miss out on that little lecture?"

"Easy," Molly replied. "I told them I was seeing someone."

"Are you?"

Molly shrugged. Her smile slipped a notch. "I was. Sort

of. But things haven't worked out. I'm thinking about taking a job in Louisiana."

Katie sensed there was more to the story than her friend was letting on, but from Molly's closed expression, she decided to back off.

"Enough about me," Molly said, her mood lightening. "How's Operation Baby coming along?"

Katie frowned. "Slowly. It hasn't been as easy as I thought it would be. Remember the medical equipment salesman I told you about?"

Molly nodded.

"He turned out to be married with a family."

"The dirty scum ball."

"My thoughts exactly," Katie returned, moved by her friend's indignation on her behalf. "But I still have Paulo and Scott. Hopefully I'll be able to choose one of them."

"The Spanish professor and the stockbroker?" Molly asked.

"Right. I've gone out with them a couple of times, but I decided to take things slower and wait until Sean finishes his background checks on them."

"Sounds smart to me." Molly paused. "But I still say if you're determined to do this, it would make more sense to choose someone you already know and trust. For instance, someone like my cousin."

Katie's heart pounded at just the thought of making love with Sean, of having his child. "Don't be ridiculous."

"What's so ridiculous about it? The two of you aren't exactly strangers. You've known him most of your life. Besides, from what my aunt said I sort of got the impression things might be getting serious between you two."

Katie flushed. Her fingers tightened around her glass of lemonade. "I can't imagine why Mrs. F. would say something like that, or why you would believe it. Everyone knows that Sean and I are just friends.''

Silence hung between them for long seconds. ''Actually, it wasn't Sean I was referring to,'' Molly said. ''I was talking about Michael. I was under the impression that the two of you had been seeing each other.''

Katie could feel her face heating. She wanted to crawl under the table and hide from the speculative look in Molly's eyes. Instead she took a sip of lemonade. It could have been dishwater for all she knew because she couldn't even taste it. ''Michael and I went out a few times, but it was never anything serious. We enjoyed each other's company, but that's all. We decided we were better off as friends. The chemistry just wasn't there between us.''

''Unlike with you and Sean.''

''Put away the detective face, Molly. You're off base.''

''Am I?''

''Yes,'' Katie replied emphatically. ''Sean and I are friends.''

''Katie, you may be my best friend, but you don't lie worth a damn.'' When Katie started to protest, Molly said, ''Come on. This is me, remember? I'm the one who helped you ambush that cousin of mine with snowballs when we were ten. I'm the one whose shoulder you cried on when you were thirteen and decided you wanted to marry him after he taught you how to kiss, only to have him break your heart by chasing after that little witch Kimberly.''

''Molly…'' Katie pleaded, not wanting to rehash her adolescent dreams and embarrassments.

''Tell me the truth, Katie. Are you in love with him?''

''I don't want to discuss this,'' Katie said firmly, afraid if she said it aloud, then it would be true.

''Come on. You can tell me. You know you can. We

always told each other everything. Didn't I let you pierce my ears?''

''And we both ended up at the doctor's office with crooked holes and blood oozing down our necks.''

Molly grinned. ''It made us blood sisters. And as your blood sister, there's nothing you can't tell me.''

''I hate to interrupt what sounds like a fascinating and enlightening conversation,'' Sean said, a note of amusement in his voice.

Katie found herself wanting to crawl beneath the picnic table. But then a pair of strong hands came down on her shoulders, squeezed gently, and her pulse started doing somersaults.

''How about taking a hike, Cuz? I need to talk to Katie.''

''Go right ahead,'' Molly replied sweetly, flashing her cousin a cheeky grin. ''I don't mind.''

''Yeah. But I do,'' Sean told her. ''Now scram. I want to talk to Katie without an audience.''

Six

"Sean!"

Katie started to rise, but Sean kept his hands on her shoulders, holding her in place. "Goodbye, Cuz," he told Molly.

"You don't have to go," Katie protested.

"It's all right. I need to talk to Michael, anyway. Behave yourself, Cuz," Molly instructed him as she swung her legs over the bench seat and stood.

"Don't I always?" Sean replied.

"You don't really want me to answer that, do you?" she asked. "If he gives you any trouble, just yell," she told Katie, before sauntering off to join Michael who was in an argument about the last Cubs game.

"Fascinating conversation you and my cousin were having," Sean teased. Still standing behind her, he couldn't quite see her face, but a flush raced up Katie's neck. "It's impolite to eavesdrop."

"Yeah, but so much fun," he whispered in her ear. "Especially when it makes you blush so prettily." Just as he had hoped, another streak of color climbed her lovely neck. After not seeing or talking with Katie for the past ten days, he found himself sorely tempted to press a kiss to that pale, silky skin. But noting the stiffness of her shoulders beneath his palms, he thought it best not to push his luck, and released her.

Moving to Katie's left, Sean straddled the end of the bench she occupied and stared into those wide, cautious, brown eyes. Not for the first time he wished he knew what was going on inside of her head. She'd been as skittish as a colt, the night she'd kicked him out of her apartment, laying on the friendship talk as thick as maple syrup and talking a mile a minute. He'd shaken her. He knew that. Hell, he'd shaken himself, Sean admitted. He certainly hadn't expected to find himself in the grip of a powerful lust attack with Katie—and certainly not after she'd made it as clear as glass that she wanted nothing from him but friendship.

But he seemed to be having a heck of a time thinking of her as just a friend these days. The interesting twist was that he'd half expected Katie to take his head off for the liberties he'd taken. The last thing he'd expected her to do was run. The Katie Malloy he knew never ran from anything. Her feminist soul wouldn't hear of it. Yet he couldn't shake the nagging suspicion that running was exactly what she was doing.

His gaze dropped to her mouth, and that tight fist of need tugged at him again. Suddenly Sean had an image of Katie as she had been that night on the couch—with her eyes all smoky, her lips swollen and parted, her small breasts ripe and begging for his touch.

"It was rude of you to tell Molly to get lost that way."

Giving himself a mental shake, Sean made a lazy journey back up to her face and smiled at her disapproving expression. "Yeah, but it worked. Didn't it?"

"It was still rude," she insisted.

"So, she can arrest me."

Katie arched a brow. "Careful," she said, the hint of a smile teasing the corners of her mouth. "Knowing Molly, she just might."

"You could be right," Sean admitted, as he considered his cousin the cop. "But a night in jail would still be worth it. After all, I got what I wanted—you all to myself."

Katie laughed out loud, and the sound rippled over him. It was the first time he'd heard the sound in weeks, and he realized he missed hearing Katie laugh. "Have you looked around, Fitzpatrick? There's at least seventy-five people here."

"Hey, what can I say? I'm a desperate man. If ten minutes in my parents' backyard is the only way I can have a conversation with you, then I'll settle for what I can get."

"What on earth are you talking about? We're neighbors, remember? We see and talk to each other all the time."

"Not lately we don't," he reminded her. "Truth is, I thought maybe you were avoiding me."

Katie shifted her gaze to the glass of lemonade, but not before he caught that guilty look in her eyes. She was so easy to read sometimes, it really was sweet. "I don't know where you got an idea like that from," she said, in what he suspected was intended to be an innocent voice.

Good thing she had opted to teach nursery school, Sean thought, because an actress Katie wasn't. "Oh, maybe it had something to do with the fact that I've seen you for all of about five minutes in the past ten days."

"You've been out of town," she reminded him. "And I…well, I've been busy."

"Yeah. I've noticed," Sean said with a frown. "You've been as busy as a little bee ever since that night in your den when I kissed your socks off. And I have to tell you, Malloy, it's hell on a guy's ego to have a woman melt like butter in his arms one minute and then avoid him like the plague for the next ten days."

Katie's head whipped up and she fired a militant glare at him. "First off, it would take a nuclear explosion to dent your ego, Sean Fitzpatrick. But just so you'll know, I am not avoiding you. Because contrary to what you believe, I did not melt like butter in your arms, and you did not kiss my socks off. I wasn't even wearing socks."

Sean grinned, and gave in to the pleasure of checking out her legs again. "You're right—about the socks, I mean. You weren't wearing any. In fact, as I recall, you weren't wearing much of anything."

The look she gave him could have turned flames to ice. "You're despicable."

"That's not the way you were feeling when you were lying under me on that couch and kissing me back," he taunted just to see her blush again. "Which brings us back to the fact that you have been avoiding me. I want to know why."

"Oh, for Pete's sake, I have not been avoiding you. I told you. I've just been really busy."

"Morning and night?"

"Yes," she snapped.

"You were home when I got in last night. I saw your car, but you didn't answer when I knocked on your door."

"I must have already been asleep. I've been going into the nursery early. We're working on some new projects for the summer for the kids. I guess I was so tired last night that I didn't hear you."

Sure you were, Sean thought, but he decided to let it

pass and not remind her that he knew that she was a light sleeper. Nor did he remind her that she had never, to his knowledge, been a person who went to bed with the chickens no matter how long of a day she'd put in. It was one of the many things the two of them had in common. "So, I'm imagining things? You really haven't been trying to avoid me?"

"Absolutely not."

"Then how come you took off for here today without me? We usually drive to the barbecue together."

"How was I to know you wanted us to ride together?"

"We always come to this shindig together," he reminded her.

"Not always," she argued, defiance gleaming in those brandy-dark eyes. "Maybe most of the time, but not always." Her fingers trembled slightly before she closed them around the glass. "Besides, how was I supposed to know? You might have made other plans, and I would have been an intrusion."

Sean frowned. He'd stake a bottle of Irish whisky that there was some kind of feminine double-talk going on here. Problem was, as much as he liked the fairer sex, he didn't have a clue as to the way their minds worked. And he didn't have a clue as to what Katie was trying to tell him now. All he knew was that she was as nervous as a long-tailed cat in a room filled with rockers. "I didn't ask anyone to come with me today, if that's what you mean. But even if I had, you wouldn't have been an intrusion. We're supposed to be friends."

"We are friends," she said, grabbing the word like a lifeline. "And because we're friends, we're not going to let anything change that. Right?"

"Right," Sean replied cautiously, unsure where this was leading.

"I mean, neither one of us is going to let a few kisses that got out of hand for a few minutes one night mess up our friendship. Right?"

"Of course not."

"I mean, it was no big deal. Really. I mean, nothing really happened."

Sean decided not to comment on that one. Enough had happened that he thought he might like to seriously reconsider the boundaries of their friendship.

"So, I don't want you to worry about that...um...kiss. I mean, I didn't read anything into it, and I'm sure you didn't either."

"All right," he said, still feeling a bit confused. Was her attack of nerves, all her avoidance of him, because of that kiss?

"Well," she said, her fingers fluttering up and down the glass. She gave him what had to be the world's biggest counterfeit smile. "Now that we've got that out of the way, I want to hear all about your trip to New Orleans. How was it? Is the place really as wicked as they say it is?"

"The trip was fine. New Orleans was hot and humid, and I was too busy tracking down a witness to check out the sin factor. Katie—"

"Someday I'd like to go there," she said, evidently on a roll because she showed no signs of slowing down. Her mouth was moving at breakneck speed again. "It seems like such an interesting place to visit. So much history, so much—"

"I'll take you someday."

She blinked. "You will? That's so sweet of you," she said, barely stopping long enough to catch a breath. She continued to ramble on about New Orleans and the things she wanted to see there, while she kept shooting him those "we're pals" smiles and fidgeted and flittered like a hummingbird's wings.

"Now that you're back, I'm hoping you'll have time to finish those investigations for me. I know Eric was a disappointment, and I feel like a real idiot for not seeing the obvious. But I have a really good feeling about Paulo and Scott. I'm sure neither of them will be a problem. And I'm hoping you'll be able to just wrap up their background checks. Do you think you'll be able to finish those investigations anytime soon? I'm really anxious to get moving with my plans."

Mention of her plan to get pregnant hit Sean like a bucket of ice water. He snagged the fingers toying with her lemonade glass and imprisoned them in his own. When both her hands and mouth were still, Sean asked, "Are we finished playing Twenty Questions yet?"

"Twenty Questions?"

Sean sighed. "Come on, Malloy. This is me, remember? I know you, honey. Something's wrong. Why don't you just tell me what it is?"

"I don't know what you mean," she said, her voice husky, her eyes wary.

"I mean, you've been chattering and fidgeting like a ditsy female for the past ten minutes. The only time I've ever seen you act that way is when something's bothering you."

"I am not behaving like a ditsy female," she informed him and tugged her hands free. "And nothing is bothering me."

"Then why in the devil won't you even look at me? And why are you pretending nothing happened between us, when we both know damned well that something did?"

She turned, met his gaze head-on. "Of course I know

something happened between us. Didn't I just say as much?''

"No. What you did was give me some song and dance about chemistry. The last time, you blamed it on wine and hormones. I'm not buying either number." Not when it turned the woman he'd always admired and cared for into a skittish female, uncomfortable in his company.

"It's the truth," she replied as though she were a teacher and he was her not-too-bright pupil. "If I seem nervous, it's because...because doggone it, Fitzpatrick, we're friends. I don't want to mess things up between us, and I think the best thing for us both to do is to forget about that kiss and concentrate on being friends."

Sean caught Katie by the nape and brought her face within a whisper of his own. "Katie, darling," he said, his voice sharp despite the endearment. "Do us both a favor. Stop tossing that word *friend* at me." The unspoken *or else* hung in the air between them.

"But we are friends, we—"

"Katie," he warned.

Her eyes went all dark and liquid, and Sean felt the painful swelling against his jeans. "Or else what?" she asked in a voice that had gone as smoky as her eyes.

"Or else I haul you into my lap, right here, right now, and I kiss you in front of my family and everyone until I knock the socks off both of us."

"But we're friends."

"Is friendship enough for you?" he asked.

Because right now friendship didn't seem nearly enough for him. Not when he could smell her flower-scented skin, feel the pulse beating in her neck. Not when he wanted to taste her sassy mouth, taste every silken inch of her. Not when he wanted to press her down on the picnic table, on the grass, against a tree, anywhere, everywhere, and feel her beneath him, hear her making those sweet, satisfied noises deep in her throat when he filled her.

"Is friendship enough?" he repeated.

But even as he asked the question, he was scared spitless. If she said no, that friendship was not enough, that she wanted more, that she wanted him, he was afraid that he would hurt her. Worse, he was terrified that he would disappoint her. Heaven help him, he didn't want to disappoint her.

"It has to be," she said finally. "I want...I need you to be my friend."

Her response slashed through him, left an acid taste in his mouth. Maybe she had been right when she'd accused him of having an ego. Evidently he did, because he didn't want to believe her. He wanted to prove to her she was wrong. But ego or not, he hadn't been mistaken about her response to him when they had kissed—regardless of what she claimed.

The problem was that despite all her protests about giving up on fairy tales and magic and white knights, Katie wanted the fairy-tale prince. Heck, she deserved it. Only he had never been white knight or prince material. He only knew that for Katie he wanted to try. And the realization that he wanted to try made his knees weak and scared him silly.

Katie's heart beat frantically as she searched Sean's face, waited for his reaction. For a moment she held her breath, sure he was going to call her a liar and make good on his threat to drag her into his lap and kiss her. And for a moment, one tiny moment of complete madness, she almost wanted him to. Because despite what she'd told him, she was very much afraid she was falling in love with him—

something she had promised herself she wasn't going to do.

Sean dropped his hand to his side. Shutters seemed to slam down on those incredible blue eyes. "All right. If that's what you want," he said, and scooted back, putting more distance between them.

It was what she wanted. Wasn't it? Then why had disappointment lodged thick in her throat at his response? "Then we're okay?" Katie asked, doing her best to sound cheerful.

"Sure," Sean replied. "We're fine."

Then why did she feel this awful sadness, this loneliness inside? Why did she want to throw her arms around him, kiss him, and tell him she'd changed her mind?

Because she was an idiot, Katie told herself. A little sexual attraction did not equal love. And Sean didn't love her—not in that way. She was his friend. Nothing more.

"Hey, Sean," Michael yelled. "Get your ugly butt over here."

When he hesitated, Katie said, "Go on. You'd better see what he wants."

"Right," he said. "Otherwise, he's liable to get nasty."

"Michael? Nasty? I don't believe it."

"Believe it," he said, pushing up from the bench. He paused. "Catch you later?"

"Sure." And when he caught up with her later, Katie promised herself, as she watched him jog off to join his brother, she would have all these crazy, dangerous feelings for Sean tucked safely away where they belonged. Swinging her legs over the side of the bench, she abandoned her seat. As she went in search of Molly, she told herself again that she'd made the right decision. Sean needed her friendship, and she needed his. And she absolutely, positively refused to let her foolish heart fall in love with him.

* * *

Blast her untrustworthy heart, Katie fumed less than an hour later, as Sean scanned the area and brought his gaze to rest on her. He winked at Katie, and her treacherous heart started fluttering with hope.

"You all right, Katie, dear?" Mrs. Fitzpatrick asked.

"Fine," she lied. How could she be fine when she was falling hard and fast for Sean? It was as plain as the detested freckles across her nose. Why else when the conversation with her mother, Mrs. F., Molly and Ryan's wife, Clea, turned to babies had her gaze automatically sought out Sean? And why else when she'd proclaimed her decision not to marry but to have a baby, did the image of a little dark-haired bundle with Sean's blue eyes pop into her head?

"You with us, Katie?" Molly asked, a knowing gleam in her eyes.

"Sure." Or at least she would be—just as soon as she could remember what the conversation had been about.

As though reading her thoughts, Molly said, "You were saying something about the notion being archaic that a woman has to get married to be happy."

"That's right," Katie chimed in, grateful for her friend's prompting. "It is. I don't have anything against the institution. I just don't think it's for everyone. And I don't see any reason why a woman should have to give up something as fulfilling as having a baby simply because she doesn't have a husband."

"Poppycock," Mrs. F. proclaimed with a shake of her head. "A child needs both parents. How do you think my boys would have turned out without me and their father to raise them?"

"I suspect they would have turned out just fine. But not everyone is as lucky as you and Mr. F. Not all marriages are as strong as yours."

"More poppycock! Marriages take work. Lots of it. Why, you wouldn't believe some of the fights my Keegan and I used to have. Still do for that matter," she said with a glint in her eyes that reminded Katie so much of Sean's. "The key to any marriage is knowing when and where to make up. As far as I'm concerned, the best place for both is in bed."

"Bragging, Aunt Isabel?" Molly asked cheekily.

Isabel Fitzpatrick shook a finger at her niece. "You're another one with too many ideas about what a woman does and doesn't need," she said, but the smile on her lips betrayed any real censure.

Katie smiled at the tiny, dark-haired woman who had given birth to four impossibly handsome sons and still shared a passionate relationship with her husband of thirty-seven years. "Like I said, not everyone is as lucky as you, Mrs. F."

"I certainly wasn't," Katie's own mother added. "I only had a few years with Katie's father before he took off. And Adam and Peter weren't much better. But the one good thing that came out of that first marriage was my Katie. I'd trade ten husbands before I'd rewrite the past if it meant me not having my daughter. Katie's a smart girl. I trust her to do what she feels is right."

"You're as batty as your daughter, Alice. You should have given Henry the boot long before he left you, and you never should have married those other two losers."

"I loved them," her mother admitted. And so had Katie. But love hadn't been enough to hold them.

Isabel Fitzpatrick sighed. "I know you did, honey. And that's what this is about. Love. Katie here is the product of the love you and Henry shared. And that's what a baby should be. The creation of two people's love—not a means to fulfill a woman's maternal instincts."

The words hit Katie like an open-palmed slap. Was that what she was doing? Fulfilling a maternal instinct? She hadn't thought so. She genuinely wanted a child. But she had never thought of a baby as two people's love. She had never thought of herself that way either.

Sure, she had missed not having a father growing up, but she'd always felt loved by her mother. And, of course, the Fitzpatricks had always been there for her—Molly offering her a shoulder to cry on, Sean and his brothers defending her and giving stern warnings to her potential boyfriends. Even Mr. Fitzpatrick had filled in as a temporary father when she'd needed one for the father-daughter luncheon at school. She knew she had good intentions, but would she be doing her baby an injustice by bringing him or her into a world without two parents who loved each other?

"What Katie needs is to find herself the right man, marry him and then have herself a houseful of babies. That's what my Ryan's done," she said, and gave a pat to her daughter-in-law's bulging stomach. "I just pray the rest of my boys settle down soon and start making me grandbabies while I'm still around to enjoy them."

"Well, if your boys had a lick of sense, one of them would have realized what a gem my Katie is and married her, and we'd both be enjoying grandbabies."

"Maybe they would have if Katie had given them an ounce of encouragement—"

"You know, I'm awfully thirsty," Katie said, shoving back her chair to stand. She wanted no part of the scenario unfolding. "I think I'll go get some more lemonade."

"I think I'll join you," Molly said.

"Me, too," Clea chimed in, and the three of them escaped, leaving the two old friends to argue over the merits and intelligence of their children.

As they walked over to the makeshift bar, Katie, once

again, found herself searching the grounds for Sean. As though he could feel her watching him, he turned his head and met her gaze.

"You look like you're about to pop," Molly told Clea, breaking into Katie's thoughts.

"I feel like I'm about to pop," Clea Fitzpatrick told them and waddled over to sit down.

Katie stared at the woman who had stolen the youngest Fitzpatrick's heart. With dark hair and pale skin, Clea wasn't drop-dead gorgeous, but she radiated a quiet beauty. To everyone's surprise, she and Ryan had had a whirlwind courtship that started with him working as her bodyguard and culminated with their wedding. Now they were expecting their first child—a miracle baby because of Clea's medical history. And Katie couldn't help but envy her a little. How wonderful it must be to marry the man you love and find yourself pregnant with his baby, Katie thought.

"I couldn't help but notice you with Sean earlier," Clea told her. "You two seem very...close."

"We're good friends," Katie replied, and took a hasty sip of her lemonade.

"Some of the best romances start out as friendships," she replied. "To be honest, when Sean was looking at you earlier, it didn't look to me like he had friendship on his mind."

"Knowing my cousin, I doubt that Sean ever looks at a woman and thinks of just friendship," Molly offered.

"Well, you're both wrong. Sean and I are just good friends."

"I'm sorry if I embarrassed you. I didn't mean to. The attraction between you just seemed so obvious," Clea replied.

"You misinterpreted our relationship," Katie assured her. "Sean is attracted to all women."

"Really? I know Sean's a flirt. All of the Fitzpatrick men are, but I never thought of Sean as a womanizer."

"Oh, he's not," Katie assured her. "I mean, he would never use a woman or anything like that. He likes them too much, and the ladies like him."

"What about you?" Clea asked her. "Do you like him?"

"Pretty hard not to," Katie admitted. "I guess it's a good thing, we're not each other's type. He likes simpering blondes with IQs that match their bra size, and I…I prefer a man who isn't threatened by a woman who can think for herself."

"I'm probably going to sound like I'm defending my brother-in-law, but I never got the impression that Sean was the type of man who would try to hold a woman back."

"He's not, but the man is stubborn, and we argue a lot."

"It's true," Molly added. "Those two have been at each other since they were kids. Of course, I've always suspected Sean baited Katie because he had a crush on her."

Katie glared at her friend. "Traitor. You know as well as I do that Sean just likes to try and boss me around. He thinks he knows better than I do what's best for me."

Clea smiled, a secret feminine smile. "Oh, I'm familiar with that particular vice. Ryan has it, too. Must be a family trait."

"Must be," Katie murmured. "All I know is that when Sean starts telling me what I should do or what's wrong with my way of thinking, we end up at each other's throats."

There was that smile again. "Didn't you hear my mother-in-law? The best part of fighting with a man is making up. Maybe you and Sean should try it."

Katie was saved from having to answer by an ear-piercing whistle that sliced through the air.

"All right, everybody. Listen up," Michael yelled. "It's time to get down to the real reason all of you were invited here today." His expression serious, he scanned the faces of the dozens of family and friends scattered about the yard.

"Oh, for the love of St. Patty, get on with it, son," Keegan Fitzpatrick shouted to his son. "Just tell the folks it's time to play football and get it done with. I'm growing older by the minute waiting for you to finish your fancy speech making."

Everyone laughed, including Michael and Sean. "You heard my pop," Michael said. "It's time for the annual football game. Anyone over the age of sixteen who wants to play be at the big oak tree in ten minutes. Sean and I are team captains, and we'll be picking our players."

"Malloy," Sean called out to her from across the yard and motioned for her to join them. "Come on."

She couldn't help it. Katie's heart started jitterbugging again when he smiled at her. She turned to Clea. "Do you mind? I haven't missed one of these games since I was old enough to play."

"Go ahead. Both of you. I'll be fine."

"You sure?" Molly asked.

"I'm posit— Oh, my. Who is that?"

Katie turned and looked in the direction where Clea was staring. Her heart slammed against her ribs and stopped. Pain sliced through her. Standing under the oak tree in front of God, the Fitzpatricks and everyone was Heather Harrison, with her arms wrapped around Sean's neck, her centerfold body pressed closer to him than butter on bread, and her lips locked on his in one doozy of a kiss.

Seven

Sean grabbed Heather's wrists and pried them from around his neck, then managed to break the lip lock she had on his mouth. "Heather," he said through clenched teeth. "What in the devil do you think you're doing?"

"Saying hello," the shapely blonde informed him.

"No. I mean, what are you doing *here?*"

"Surprised?" she replied, smiling, a sultry expression on her face. "I hoped you would be. I called your mother and explained how you'd asked me to come with you, but that I had to turn you down because I was supposed to be out of town for a fitness forum on the West Coast."

Sean vaguely recalled mentioning the family affair to Heather a couple of months ago—when he'd been in the heavy throes of first lust. But that had been before...before Katie. Or rather before his relationship with Katie had shifted directions. The casual invitation to Heather, along with any romantic or sexual interest he'd had in the woman, had been filed away under fond memories. He sure as heck didn't want Heather here now, climbing all over him and giving everyone the impression that the two of them had a thing going. It wasn't Heather he wanted. It was Katie.

Katie! He darted his gaze across the yard to where he'd last seen her. "Aw, hell," he muttered. Sure enough, Katie hadn't missed Heather's lip attack. And he could just imagine what she was thinking. Probably the same thing Michael had accused him of—changing women like he changed socks.

It wasn't true, of course. But fat chance he'd have convincing her of that. Sure, he had been in love more than once. What man over thirty hadn't? But he had never claimed to be a monk when it came to the opposite sex. He loved big, lusted big and fell hard every time. And he made sure the lady in question got as much as she gave. What he didn't do, what he had never done and never would do, was play games with a woman's feelings. And as far as he was concerned, he'd thought he had ended things with Heather long before he'd found himself on that couch with Katie, generating enough steam to power a locomotive. Obviously the message he'd delivered to Heather hadn't been clear.

"Sean, honey, is anything wrong?"

"Heather, I think we need to have a little talk." He may have toyed with the idea of being noble and keeping things on a friends-only basis with Katie as she had asked, or at least he wanted to think he would have given it a try. But the fact was his feelings for Katie were anything but noble, and they certainly weren't what he could call friendly. It would be unfair to Heather to pretend otherwise or to use her as a substitute.

"You upset with me for coming?" she asked, her bee-stung lips forming a perfect pout that should have had him itching to kiss her, but didn't.

"Nah," he said, leading her away from curious eyes. "I'm not upset with you, darling, but I do want to make sure we understand each other."

Fifteen minutes later Sean was fairly sure he'd gotten through to Heather that the relationship between them was over. Although he had a sneaking suspicion the woman planned to do her best to change his mind. Probably some female, point-of-pride thing, he figured. Either way, he hadn't had the heart to refuse when she'd asked him if she could stay.

"Hey, lover boy," Michael called to him. "You gonna play football or not?"

"I'm playing," Sean replied, grateful for the chance to escape Heather. Besides, he was looking forward to teaming up with Katie for the football game.

"All right. Call it while it's in the air. Heads or tails," Michael said as he flipped the coin in the air.

"Tails."

"Heads it is. I get first pick." Michael smiled, and his eyes, a paler shade of blue than Sean's own, glinted wickedly as he exchanged a look with their other brother Ryan. Sean didn't like that look, and he liked it even less when Michael crooked a finger in Katie's direction. "Over here, Malloy."

"Hey, wait a minute," Sean protested. He glared at his older brother. "You know Katie's always on my team."

"Not today she isn't," Michael informed him, his lips curving in a smug grin. He draped a protective arm around Katie's shoulders. "Come on, love. How'd you like to help me and the rest of our team beat the pants off of my little brother?"

"I think I'd enjoy that," Katie said with an answering grin.

They continued selecting players, and by the time they'd finished divvying up the teams, Sean was in a nasty mood—in part because Michael had stolen Katie, his best receiver, from him, and in part because Katie hadn't seemed to mind one bit. And while he had been worried about Katie's reaction to Heather's presence, she evidently didn't think it was any big deal. It certainly would have been a big deal to him if Eric or one of those other bozos she'd been dating had come to the barbecue and lip wrestled with her.

"Sean, what about Heather?" Katie asked. "Do you think she wants to play?"

"In that outfit?" Ryan tossed back.

Once again Sean couldn't help but notice the difference between the two women. Night and day, he thought. Heather, in her skin-hugging white shorts, snug-fitting halter top and sandals, was a stunner, and any normal, red-blooded male would have been panting just looking at her. But it was Katie in her weathered sweatshirt, worn cutoffs and sneakers that had him aching to throw her across his shoulder and carry her off to the nearest bed and make love to her.

"I do believe you're right, Cuz," Molly replied. "I don't think football is the game the lady came to play."

"Cut it out, you guys," Katie chided. "What about it, Sean? You want to ask her to join us?"

It was just like Katie to worry that they'd hurt his feelings. "Nah. Heather used to be a cheerleader," Sean said, in the other woman's defense. "She's going to cheer my team to victory."

But more than two hours later, Heather's cheerleading didn't seem to be working. With the score tied at twenty, all of Sean's attention should have been focused on the pigskin in Michael's hands—and not on the sassy-eyed auburn-haired woman sporting a skinned knee, a streak of dirt down one cheek and grass stains across her skinny backside. Suddenly he realized that cute backside was moving, and Sean jerked his attention to Michael who had sent the football screaming through the air like a missile. And that missile was headed for Katie.

Sean broke into a run. Adrenaline pumping through him, he raced downfield toward the end zone. Within moments, he was closing in on Katie to intercept the ball. Determination etched in every line of her face, she pumped her long legs, eating up the yards fast. But his legs were longer, Sean thought smugly. She'd never be able to make the catch. And he was going to have himself a beauty of an interception.

Shooting him a deadly glance, Katie cut back and leaped up in front of him to grab the ball. Screams exploded around them as she pulled the ball down, tucked it into her body and then started to run.

Caught off guard by the move, Sean swung around and raced after her. He lunged for Katie just as she started to cross the goal line, tackling her around the middle and tumbling her down to the ground.

A roar of whoops and shouts went up. He heard someone yell "touchdown," and could have sworn he heard Heather's disappointed whine. Then everything and everyone seemed to simply disappear. Everything shut down around him until his world encompassed only him and Katie. He could hear the sound of their ragged breathing, feel the movement of her chest as it rose and fell with each labored breath, smell the sweat and grass. He felt her soft body sprawled beneath his, her breasts just a flex away from his palms, the ridge of his sex nudged against her bottom.

Any remote ideas he still had about being noble and holding to the friends-only mandate Katie claimed to want bit the dust. Friendship wasn't what was on his mind now. Katie was. He wanted her. Right here. Right now. Naked and eager beneath him.

"Uh, Sean, you can let me up now," Katie said, her voice the same throaty whisper he remembered from that night in her apartment when he'd come so close to making love to her. When he didn't answer, simply held her tighter and closed his eyes, she said, "Sean. I really think you should get off me."

"Right. Sorry," he muttered. Pushing to his feet, he offered Katie a hand up. "Great catch," he told her, reluctant to let go of her hand. He wanted to wipe the smudge from her cheek, trail his finger across the freckles on her nose. And he wanted to kiss that soft mouth.

"Thanks," she said, tugging her hand free from his.

Michael ripped Katie from his arms, lifted her up and swung her around. "You were incredible," he said, giving her a kiss full on the mouth.

Ryan swooped over to claim Katie the minute Michael set her down. "He's right. You were magnificent, Katie! If I weren't a happily married man, I swear I'd ask you to marry me."

Sean gritted his teeth. "We going to play ball or what?"

They played ball, and the remainder of the game was an exercise in frustration for Sean. As Michael's favorite receiver, Katie continued to carry the ball. Assigned to defend against another touchdown strike, he was the one forced to tackle her. And each time he tumbled to the ground with Katie beneath him, Sean's nerves grew that much closer to the edge.

The game finally ended with Michael's team leading by seven points, when his mother insisted everyone stop and sample the homemade ice cream. For the thirty minutes that Katie stuck around, she was all sunshine and warmth and the picture of friendship. He'd have bought the whole thing if he hadn't caught her sneaking glances at him when she thought he wasn't looking, and if he hadn't remembered the way she'd kissed him. There had been a hell of a lot more than friendship in those kisses, regardless of what she claimed. He'd have called her on it, too, proved it to both of them, were it not for the problem of Heather.

When Katie gave some flimsy excuse about laundry and made a beeline for her car, Sean excused himself and went after her. "Katie, wait a second," Sean called, catching her as she unlocked her car door.

"What's up?" she asked, but he could see the nervousness in her eyes now that they were alone.

"I was wondering if you wanted to get together for some dinner later. You know, and catch up a bit."

"Gee, I'd like to, Sean. Really I would, but I've made plans for tonight."

"A date?" Sean threw out the question before he could stop himself.

"As a matter of fact, yes."

"Not Hartmann."

"Are you crazy?" she asked. "No way would I go out with that slime again."

"Then who?"

"Paulo Santiago. You remember, he's the Spanish professor I told you about."

"One of your daddy candidates," he said, frowning, and decided that as soon as he got into his office in the morning Paulo Santiago would have the full benefit of his attention.

"I thought you were going to hold off on that plan until I'd had a chance to check him out."

"I'm just having dinner with him, Sean. I think I can manage that without your report."

"Yeah. You're right," Sean said, running a hand through his hair. "But I was hoping to have a chance to talk to you this evening. I wanted to explain about Heather."

"Hey, you don't need to explain anything to me. I'm happy things have worked out the way you wanted."

"Yeah, well, that's just it," he tried to explain. "I mean Heather and I...we...we're not really together—not the way you think."

"Don't worry, I'm sure she'll come around. I haven't known a girl yet who could resist that Fitzpatrick charm." She patted his cheek and gave him that infernal "we're friends" smile. "If you still want to talk to me about it later, you know you can. But right now I really do have to go if I'm going to get my laundry done before Paulo arrives."

Then she was gone. And he was left standing on the curb in front of his family's home, wondering how a man who'd never before in his life had problems talking to a woman could suddenly have such a difficult time explaining to Katie that he wasn't interested in talking to her about Heather or anyone else. Because he wasn't interested in anyone else—only Katie. The only woman he really wanted was Katie. And despite that famous Fitzpatrick charm, she seemed set on their remaining just friends.

"You know, Katherine, with just a little more practice, you would be able to speak Spanish like a native," Paulo told her three nights later.

"You really think so?" Katie asked as she took a sip of her cappuccino and tried to muster some enthusiasm for the man's praise and his company. In truth, her mind wasn't on Paulo or on perfecting her Spanish. It was on Sean. Try as she might, she didn't seem to be doing a very good job of keeping the man out of her thoughts. But at least his being out late the last few nights had helped her gain some perspective and helped to bolster her resolve. Sean was her friend. The guy needed a friend he could talk turkey with, and she was determined to be that friend if it killed her.

"Yes, I do. As a matter of fact, I have been thinking about making a trip to Spain after the summer school term ends next month. I would like you to come with me," he said, in that seductive accent that she had to admit was charming.

"You want me to go to Spain with you?"

He gave her a slow, enticing smile that she'd seen send more than one female in her class into a tizzy. "Yes. At least, we would go to Spain initially." He captured her hands and brought them to his mouth and kissed her fingers. He gazed up at her and said, "I would also like to show you Italy, especially Venice. Such romantic countries, a perfect place for lovers."

Katie stared at the man nibbling on her fingers. Six weeks ago she had considered asking him to father a child with her. He was still every bit as handsome—wavy, dark hair tinged with pewter at the temples, olive complexion that bespoke his Spanish heritage and black eyes that had a way of looking at a girl and making her feel like a goddess. He was still single—something she had made darned sure about this time—kind, patient, a perfect gentleman. He was fluent in three languages—two more than she—and he spoke adoringly of his nieces and nephews, so he liked children. In terms of sex appeal, there was the added bonus of him being a foreigner with an accent that could charm the birds from the sky or a girl out of her panties. But try as she might, she couldn't muster one ounce of enthusiasm for Paulo's company—let alone the thought of spending a romantic holiday with him in Europe as her lover.

Katie pulled her hands free. "I appreciate the offer, Paulo. It sounds like an absolutely wonderful trip, but I couldn't possibly go."

"Ah, *cara*. You are worried about appearances? I assure you, it will not be a problem."

"No, it's not that," she hedged. The truth was that what people might think hadn't even crossed her mind.

"Then it is your job at the nursery school? Surely you are allowed a vacation. Yes?"

"Yes. I have vacation time coming to me. But honestly, I can't go."

"Of course you can. We will go together, and you will love Spain." He smiled at her, reached for her hand again. "I promise I will make your visit unforgettable."

Katie tucked both of her hands safely in her lap. "I'm sure you'll have an unforgettable time. But not with me. I'm not going."

His crestfallen expression did wonders for her ego. "But why, *cara?* I thought that you and I were building a relationship, that you felt something for me as I do for you."

"I like you, Paulo. Truly, I do. It's just…" Katie scrambled for an excuse that wouldn't bruise his ego but that would still let her off the hook gracefully. Finally she opted for the truth. "I can't go with you because I'm involved with someone else." She huffed out a breath and decided confession was good for her soul. "The truth is I'm in love with someone else."

"But that is not a problem, *cara*. I am in love with someone else, too. Surely just because our hearts are involved elsewhere is no reason for us to deny our mutual attraction for each other and act upon it."

Shock rendered Katie speechless—for all of ten seconds. Then fury erupted inside her, making her tremble. Shoving back from the table, she curled her hands into fists. "Actually," she said, temper making her voice drop, "I'm afraid that's plenty enough reason for me."

"But, *cara.* I don't understand."

"Then see if you understand this." Grabbing the glass of ice water in front of him, Katie dumped it in Paulo's lap, then she slapped the glass down on the table and walked out.

Twenty minutes later she slammed her car door shut and raced up the stairs to her apartment. "Must be a defective gene," she muttered as she let herself into her apartment. "First that sneak Eric, and now Paulo aka Casanova Santiago." Still furious, Katie kicked the door closed behind her.

After tossing down her keys, purse and books, she toed off her shoes and headed for the bedroom. There she ditched her skirt and blouse for a pair of boxer shorts and her oldest and most comfortable sweatshirt, then she aimed for the kitchen. Opening the freezer, she ignored the frozen TV dinners, pizzas and the vegetable lasagna she'd purchased when she'd decided she needed to eat more healthy foods. To heck with healthy, she decided. She reached for the pint of double-chocolate-chip ice cream and the jar of cherries.

Not bothering with lights, she wandered into the den and flipped on the CD player. The haunting voice of Patsy Cline belted out a mournful tune. Good old Patsy, she seemed to know all about the fickle male species, Katie thought, as she flipped the lock open to the sliding glass doors and retreated out into the darkness of the deck.

She managed to polish off nearly half the ice cream and had consigned the entire male population to the back of beyond before her temper finally began to peter out. But not even the double-chocolate-chip ice cream eased that bruised and achy feeling in her heart over Sean.

Glancing toward the quiet, dark apartment next door, Katie sighed. There was no question that Sean found her physically attractive. That much had been obvious the night they'd tangled limbs and tongues on her couch, and again last week when he'd been lying on top of her on the football field. She wasn't a complete dummy, nor was she blind to the obvious. Sean wanted her sexually—which should really have come as no surprise. He was a physical, sensual man, and Heather giving him the run-around must have been a real ego bruiser for a man like him. She could hardly blame him for responding like any normal male would when he found an eager, willing female practically climbing all over him.

Katie stabbed her spoon into the carton of ice cream. Sean had simply responded to her desire for him. Even if he had wanted her, wanting someone wasn't the same as loving them. Besides, now that dear little Heather had changed her tune, she doubted that even the physical attraction he'd felt for her would be a problem any longer—at least not for Sean. For her it was another matter entirely. The bottom line was that she loved Sean, even if he didn't love her. And because she loved him, she wanted him to be happy. If that meant him being with Heather, then she would be happy for him.

In a pig's eye, she would be happy.

Heather was all wrong for Sean. Any fool with eyes could see the woman was as shallow as a dry creek bed in a desert. Almost every time Katie'd seen her, the woman had been primping in a mirror. Heather loved herself too much to really care about Sean. And Sean, the thickheaded galoot, was evidently too blinded by lust to see that Heather

Harrison would never make him happy, would never love him—not the way that she did.

No question about it. She did have a defective gene. What else could explain her doing something as stupid as falling in love with Sean?

Disgusted with herself, Katie set the softening ice cream aside. Not even a gallon of double-chocolate-chip with a helping of cherries was going to ease what really ailed her.

Abandoning her chair, Katie walked over to the edge of the deck and leaned on the wooden railing. She stared up into the night sky. Another made-for-lovers' moon hung like a bright yellow ball in an ebony sky. Stars sprinkled across the velvety blackness, sparkling like fairy dust. Out of the corner of her eye, Katie spied one lonely star in the distance. It shimmered brilliantly for a moment, then arced and shot across the heavens. Crossing her fingers, Katie squeezed her eyes shut for a second and made a silent wish. When she opened her eyes again the star sank into the inky darkness, leaving only a trail of fading light.

"Did you make a wish?"

Katie fought back a shiver of longing as Sean's voice whispered along her nerve endings like a lover's caress. "Evidently you haven't been listening to me, Fitzpatrick," she said, striving to sound light as she turned to face him. "If you had, you'd know that the new Katie Malloy ranks wishing on stars right up there with believing in magic and fairy tales." No way did she want to admit that she had been standing here like a lovesick fool, making wishes about him that didn't have a prayer of coming true.

Sean hopped over the railing separating the two apartments. "I still say there wasn't a thing wrong with the old Katie. And there sure isn't a thing wrong with making wishes. Seems almost a shame to let a shooting star go to waste by not making one."

"You're home early tonight," Katie said, changing the subject.

"Ten o'clock isn't exactly early."

"Heather might disagree."

"I wouldn't know, since I wasn't with Heather." Sean let out a weary sigh. "I just finished up an investigation I've been working on for the last couple of days and decided to call it a night."

He'd been working, and not with Heather?

"I didn't see any lights on when I drove up and thought you'd gone to bed early—again. What are you doing out here in the dark?"

"Unwinding."

He eyed the unfinished pint of ice cream on the table and the opened jar of cherries. "Bad day?"

Katie shrugged. "I've had better."

"Want to talk about it?" Picking up the carton, he scooped out a spoonful of ice cream.

"No," she replied, and turned away from the sight of Sean cleaning the spoon with his tongue. She didn't want to think about him that way, didn't want to remember the feel of his mouth on hers. He was her friend, nothing more, she reminded herself, and stared up into the sky. The moon had disappeared behind a cluster of fast-moving clouds. The stars seemed to have lost some of their luster. Even the air had shifted from a pleasant breeze to heavy, brooding gusts that had the taste of a storm. She would like a storm. A brewing storm fitted her mood, Katie decided.

"You might feel better if you talked about it," Sean said, moving behind her.

"I don't feel bad," she fibbed.

Chuckling, Sean caught her by the shoulders and turned her around to face him. "You're a terrible liar, Malloy."

"I'm not lying."

"No? Then why's that half-empty carton of ice cream and jar of cherries sitting over there on the table?"

She hiked her chin up a notch. "Maybe I just felt like ice cream and cherries."

He caught a strand of her hair and tugged it. Then he smiled, and Katie felt that smile all the way down to her toes. "This is Sean you're talking to. I happen to know that double-chocolate-chip ice cream is your number-one comfort food. And cherries to boot, well, that means something's got you really upset. Come on, now. Fess up. Tell me what's wrong."

"Today was the pits, okay?"

"Uh-huh." He pulled her into his arms, pressed her head against his shoulder and began to stroke her back. "Tell me."

Her hard-won resolve had legs of jelly, Katie discovered, as she leaned against him. So did her foolish heart because it started singing little ditties about how Sean had been working, and not with Heather. How it was her that he was holding in his arms.

"Come on, honey. Tell me what happened."

So she told him—about the day that had started off with her oversleeping and arriving late for work, about the sick toddler who'd upchucked his lunch all over her new shoes, about having to race home and change clothes before going to class, about ending up at the coffeehouse with Paulo.

"Paulo?" Sean repeated, his shoulder tensing beneath her cheek.

"Yes, remember? I told you about him. He's the professor whose name was on my list of daddy candidates."

"Santiago," Sean said with an edge in his voice.

"Yes."

The hand stroking her hair stilled. "What did he do?"

"He didn't really do anything, except ask me to go away with him to Spain."

"You're not going," Sean told her, his voice firm. His hand tightened at her waist.

"No kidding," she replied, her earlier indignation resurfacing. "The man's a slug. He actually had the nerve to admit that he was involved—" Katie jerked her head up to see Sean's face. His mouth was drawn into a tight line. Even in the darkness she could see the anger swirling in his eyes. "Why shouldn't I go with him?"

"You said it yourself, the guy's a slug."

"Yes. He is. But you didn't know that. Not unless…" Then it dawned on her, the reason Sean was here. Not because he wanted to be with her instead of Heather. Not because he loved her as she loved him. He was here with her, holding her in his arms, out of duty. Out of friendship. "You finished your investigation on him."

"Yes."

Feeling like a fool, Katie moved away from Sean and turned once again to stare out into the night. "And?"

"And the man's a slug, just as you said. Let's just leave it at that."

"No, let's not. I want to know what you found out." At his hesitation Katie pressed. "Either tell me, or I'll find out for myself."

"He has a reputation as a real Don Juan among the female students and staff. You're not the only woman that he's romanced at the university, and you're not the first one he's asked to go away with him. He hasn't done anything illegal—"

"Just immoral."

"Yes. But all the women who've been involved with him are over twenty-one, and as far as I can determine, he's never tried to trade off grades for sex. At least no one has charged him with it if he has.''

''Pig! Now I wish I had dumped hot coffee in his lap instead of the ice water.''

''I'm sorry, Katie.''

She shrugged. ''It's not your fault. I just have lousy taste in men.''

''At least you found out now before things got serious.''

But there hadn't been any chance of things getting serious between her and Paulo or anyone else. How could there be when she was in love with Sean? ''You're right. I'm actually lucky when you think about it. I could have agreed to go with him to Spain, maybe even gotten pregnant, and then found out the man was just a roving Casanova.''

''Want me to go beat his brains out?''

And he would, she realized. She turned to face him and conjured up what she hoped passed as a smile. ''I appreciate the offer, but he's not worth the effort. Thanks, anyway, though. And thanks for letting me pour out my troubles on your shoulder.''

''Hey, you're welcome to use my shoulder anytime.''

She laughed as she was meant to, but the sound held a false note even to her own ears. ''I'll remember that. Now quit worrying over me like a mother hen and go salvage what you can of your evening.''

''What about you?''

''What do you mean?'' she asked.

''I mean what are you going to do? Are you going to call it a night?''

''In a little bit. I think I'll stay out here for a while until that storm moves in.''

Sean hesitated and eyed her closely. ''How about if I keep you company?''

But Sean was her problem. "Thanks, but I'd really like to be alone for a while," she told him, and turned away to take up her former post at the deck railing. She waited, listened for the sound of his footsteps retreating. When none came, she said, "I mean it, Sean. I really do want to be alone."

"That's too bad, because I've decided I don't want to leave."

Eight

Katie released an exasperated breath, but didn't turn around, afraid she might weaken and ask Sean to stay. "I don't need a baby-sitter, you know."

"That's good, because I'd make a lousy one." His hands came down on her shoulders, and Katie tensed. "Relax," he murmured.

"I am relaxed."

"Bull. You're wound up tighter than a spring."

It was true. Having Sean touch her, feeling the heat of his body so near her own, had the nerves in her stomach bunching up like a fist.

A dagger of lightning sliced through the sky. Thunder rumbled somewhere in the distance. The wind, heavy with the scent of rain, tugged at the hair piled atop her head and sent loose tendrils slapping across her face and mouth. The storm was close, so close she could almost taste it—the violence, the power of it. But the storm brewing inside her seemed far more threatening.

She should go inside, put distance between herself and Sean until she could get her feelings and perspective back under control.

But it was hard to pay heed to that warning voice when Sean's fingers were kneading the tight muscles in her shoulders, working magic on the knots in her neck. So, instead of doing the smart thing, instead of going inside where she would be safe from the upheaval Sean was creating in her body and her heart, Katie closed her eyes and gave in to the pleasure of his soothing touch.

His thumbs and fingers pressed, massaged, worked on muscles stiff with tension. When he pushed his thumbs to knead a particularly sore spot, Katie moaned.

"I hope that was approval."

"Definitely approval," she said on a sigh. "Hmm. That feels good."

"Glad you think so," he said, his voice a husky murmur that teased the exposed skin along the back of her neck. His hands and fingers continued to work on the knots and kinks in her shoulders, her neck, at the base of her skull. Her limbs grew liquid, almost boneless. And Katie found herself relaxing for the first time in days. As she relaxed, Sean's fingers began a new pattern of small, soothing circles in her hair, across the back of her head, along her temples.

Lightning slashed the sky again, shaking like an angry fist. Thunder followed with an equally irate grumble. Yet she made no attempt to move, wasn't even sure she could if she wanted to. Desire hummed a slow, seductive beat in her blood, and when Sean's mouth brushed her neck, it seemed like the most natural thing in the world for her to tilt her head back, to give him the access he sought.

"Ah, Katie," he said, the words whispering over her like a caress as his lips touched her collarbone. His hands slid down her arms in featherlike strokes, and when he skimmed the sides of her breasts, the air lodged in her throat. Splaying his fingers across her midriff, he gently eased her body back to rest against him. His arousal pressed against her, hard and hot, despite the clothes that separated them. This was madness, Katie told herself. Sean couldn't possibly know, he couldn't possibly have planned for his innocent massage to set off this fire of need inside her. She bit down on her bottom lip. He couldn't possibly know how close she was to begging him to touch her, to make love to her.

"Katie." Her name was a hoarse growl that fueled those fires of longing deep inside her. And then those clever hands, those oh-so-clever fingers of his, moved lower, touching her belly, playing with the edge of her sweatshirt. He sneaked beneath the worn fabric, and those big, warm and gentle hands eased up the length of her rib cage and hovered just at the base of her breasts.

Katie's breath hitched as she waited, wanting him to touch her, wanting him to ease the painful ache he'd stirred inside her. When his fingers traced the tips of her breasts, she nearly cried out. As though he could hear her silent plea, he cupped her breasts in his palms. She nearly wept as he shaped her breasts with his hands, molded her with his fingers. When he captured the tips between his thumbs and fingers and gently squeezed, she gasped, "Sean." Waves of pleasure shuddered through her and fed the spiraling need for more. "We should stop," she told him, her voice as shaky as the rest of her.

"You're right," he murmured, but he made no move to stop the exquisite havoc he was causing by touching her breasts. Instead, he bit the tender skin at her neck with his teeth, then followed with hot, wet kisses and a sweep of his tongue.

"I mean it. We've been friends too long to mess things up by doing this. We should stop."

"I agree." But one hand remained anchored to her breast while the other moved lower, retraced the path down her belly and then disappeared beneath the waistband of her shorts.

Katie tried to recall all the reasons they should not do this. But nothing in the world felt more right at the moment than being here with Sean, in his arms, his hands on her body. Her heart began that wild tango again as his fingers tunneled beneath her panties and brushed through the curls between her thighs. For long seconds she held her breath in anticipation, fearful that he would touch her and fearful that he would not. She waited for what seemed a lifetime on the precipice between want and denial. Then he dipped his fingers inside her. She whimpered and would have fallen had it not been for Sean's arm wrapped around her middle to support her. "I...I have to go inside," she told him, not sure if the thunder she heard was due to Mother Nature or her own frantically beating heart.

"Okay." But those oh-so-magical fingers of his began to move, sliding in and out, in and out, stroking, teasing the sensitive tip at the mouth of her femininity and driving her out of her mind.

Another spear of lightning ripped through the sky. Big, fat drops of rain started to fall around them. But the storm inside her had her in its grip. Sean continued to touch her intimately with slow, seductive strokes. And each time his fingers entered her, pleasured her, he drove her closer to the heart of another storm far more dangerous than the one that had the wind whipping her hair around her.

Sean thrust his fingers inside her once more, deeper this

time, demanding a response. "Don't fight it, love," he murmured. "Don't fight it."

"I—" She gripped the arm he had anchored around her middle, and when he withdrew slightly, then pushed inside her again, she went slamming into the storm. Floodgates of sensation opened, rushed through her, over her, consumed her until she could do nothing but hold on to him and cry out his name.

When the storm inside her eased, Sean whipped her around to face him. He stared at her with eyes that had gone nearly black with hunger and sent another jolt of desire rippling through her. I love you, she wanted to tell him as her knees grew weak. Afraid to say the words, afraid he wouldn't want them, she grabbed him by the collar and dragged his mouth down to hers.

Sean groaned. Then he savaged her mouth with teeth and tongue and lips while he worshiped her with his hands. He was like a starving man—insatiable—touching, tasting, taking. Finally he jerked his mouth free, and Katie could feel her knees begin to buckle.

Pressing her against the deck railing, he stepped between her legs. Then his mouth was on one breast—kissing, licking, nipping at it with his teeth. She was on fire, and the only cure for such heat had Sean's name on it. Blinded by her need to be a part of him, she reached for him again. She ripped at the buttons on his shirt, yanked it free from his pants.

He kissed her again, his tongue diving in and wiping out all thoughts, all reasoning, everything but the touch, the feel, the taste of him. She fumbled with the buckle on his belt. When her fingers brushed against his sex, he let out a low moan. She studied him with her fingers, stroking him, holding the heavy bulge in her palm and thrilled at the shudder that ran through him. Cupping her bottom, he pulled her against him, ground his hips against hers and took possession of her mouth once more.

As the storm caught her in its grip and began to drag her under a second time, the rain started to fall harder, cold and wet on her heated flesh. Lightning snapped nearby, the sound like an angry smack, while thunder roared with displeasure. Patsy's voice warbled on the CD player, only to die in the midst of another soulful note. Then the world went pitch-black.

Sean lifted his head, and she wanted to cry out in protest. "We need to get out of this rain," he told her, his voice sounding as though he'd run a marathon. His fingers bit into her shoulders as he set her away from him.

Dazed, her own breathing ragged, her heart roaring like a fast-moving train, Katie was only vaguely aware of the rain now sluicing over them, drumming on the deck. She struggled to see Sean's face in the darkness.

Had he realized just how close they'd come to making love? How near the edge she still was? She wanted to ask him why he had stopped. She didn't care about the rain. Did he? She was saved from asking the question when beams from flashlights began sprouting up from the neighboring apartments. Dragging in deep breaths, Katie's fogged senses began to clear, and she remembered all the reasons she shouldn't have allowed this to happen. Their friendship. His involvement with Heather.

"You're soaked to the skin."

"So are you."

"Yeah, but my teeth aren't chattering. You'd better go inside while I check on the power."

She didn't care about the power. She didn't care about the rain. She needed to know why he had stopped, when she knew he wanted her and she'd been more than willing.

Unless it wasn't you he wanted, a prickly voice of doubt chimed.

"Katie, I—"

One of the beams of light cut through the darkness past them, and Sean's arm went around her, drawing her close. For the space of a heartbeat, she allowed herself to enjoy the warmth of his body.

"Fitzpatrick, you over there?" Tom Drummond in the neighboring complex called out in an anxious voice. The tunnel of light bounced frantically from Sean's deck to hers, and Katie held a hand up to shield her eyes from the glare.

"Right here, Tom," Sean told him.

"Thank God. Buddy, I need your help. Erin's gone into labor. The contractions are two minutes apart. I need to get her to the hospital now, and I have to try to get hold of my mother-in-law to come stay with Tommy."

"I'll stay with Tommy," Katie offered, the emergency clearing her senses as no amount of reasoning could.

"Tell Erin to hang on. I'll grab my cell phone, and we'll call the hospital on the way," Sean told him.

Moments later as Katie settled in at the Drummonds and Sean prepared to leave with Tom and Erin for the hospital, he pulled her to him and gave her a swift kiss. "I don't know how long I'll be, but when I get back we need to talk."

Katie nodded and gave him what she hoped passed for an agreeable smile. "Now go before Erin has that baby in the car."

When he hesitated, Katie was afraid he could read the panic that had set in now that she had herself back under control. But then he turned and rushed out the door, and she wasn't sure whether to be relieved or sad.

One thing was for sure, along with the panic came more

questions. Did Sean realize it was her he'd been kissing? That it was her he had been making love to? Had he responded to her urgent need because he'd been lost in the heat of the moment? Or, like her, had he responded because he felt something more? She couldn't ask him those questions. But even if she could, she was terrified of what the answers would be.

Sean drummed his fingers on the desk and considered leaving another phone message for Katie. "Why bother?" he muttered. She hadn't returned the half-dozen messages that he'd already left her—not unless he counted those dumb voice mails she'd left him at the office saying she was sorry they kept missing each other.

"Missing each other my foot. She's flat-out avoiding me. Again." Not that he blamed her. After promising her they would talk, he'd spent the next twelve hours at the hospital with Tom. And as he'd listened to Erin Drummond's screams of pain, he vowed that he and his wife would adopt a baby—or they'd rescue a pup from the pound—before he would ever put her through the torture of bearing a child. The fact that he'd even thought of a wife had made him so dizzy he'd had to sit down. But once the sinking feeling passed, he almost laughed and wondered what Katie would say when he told her that one.

But he hadn't had a chance to tell her, to share any of it with her. Because when he'd finally returned home, little Tommy was with his grandmother and Katie had gone to work. He'd slept for the next ten hours straight, and when he'd awakened, it had been well past midnight. He had missed her again the next morning, and then he'd had to go out of town for more than a week. The case had been important. But even more important, he'd had a lead on his

brother Connor. Now eleven days had passed, and he had
yet to speak with Katie.

No. He didn't blame her for avoiding him one bit—not
after the way he'd behaved. Shoving a hand through his
hair, Sean let out a frustrated sigh. He'd come just short of
stripping Katie bare, laying her down on the deck of her
apartment and making love to her in the mother of all rainstorms.

Damn, but he'd never meant to let things get so out of
hand. Desire for her had been clawing at him for weeks—
since the day she'd come into his office telling him she was
going to have a baby. He'd never allowed himself to quite
look at Katie that way before—as a woman—not just as a
friend. But ever since he had, there had been no turning
back. Heather had become history—even if she hadn't
wanted to accept it. That's what he'd started to tell Katie
that night, when she'd looked at him out of those sad,
brown eyes filled with yearning. Then she'd tipped up that
stubborn chin, given him that phony smile and dismissed
him. He wouldn't have been able to walk away from her
then if his life had depended on it. Not after he'd spent so
many days thinking of her, missing her, wanting to be with
her. To see her smile, hear her laughter.

Faster than the blink of an eye, Katie's face loomed before him as she'd been that night. Her eyes dazed and
heavy, her mouth ripe and tempting, her body soft and
yielding. That he could respond to her as he had and have
her still believe he wanted Heather, gnawed at him. Did
she really believe him so shallow? That he would make
love to her while he lusted after another woman?

He wanted to be the man who brought magic back into
her life. But how could he when the woman was dodging
him day and night? He dragged open the desk drawers one
by one, digging beneath papers, file folders, a box of busi-

ness cards, searching for something to gnaw on, maybe a candy bar.

"Lose something?" Michael asked as he came into the office.

He struck gold—a bar of chocolate with almonds that he had bought from a neighborhood kid last fall who'd been selling boxes of the things door-to-door to raise money for a trip to D.C.

"You must be desperate if you're going to eat that."

Sean frowned at the battered candy bar. "Why?"

"Because from the looks of the wrapper, I'd say it's been in your desk for a while."

"So? Chocolate doesn't go bad." He tore off the wrapper and looked at the faded chocolate. "Does it?"

"Beats me," Michael told him, dropping a file in the center of his desk.

"Hey, wait a minute. I've already got a full caseload. Whatever that is," he said pushing the file back across the desk. "Give it to Ryan."

"We agreed not to give Ryan any cases that meant he'd have to go out of town until after Clea has the baby."

"Then you take it." Sean eyed the candy bar. Nine months wasn't that old, he reasoned, and took a bite.

"No can do. This one's yours." He pushed the file right back at Sean. "I've got too much on my plate already."

Sean swallowed. "Then hire another detective. I'm practically working around the clock as it is," he said, expecting Michael to call him down on the exaggeration.

"Need I remind you that this is a family business? Except for Dad, who's retired, there aren't any other Fitzpatricks."

"There's Connor," Sean told him, unable to let the remark pass without comment. As always, mention of his oldest brother's name brought a quiet sadness. Ignoring the

candy bar he'd been so desperate for only a moment ago,
Sean thought of his oldest brother instead. Estranged from
the family after being unjustly accused of being a dirty cop,
he'd been cleared and offered full reinstatement to duty.
But Connor had walked away, bitter and angry that their
father had doubted him. "Think he meant it about never
coming back?"

Michael sighed heavily. "It's beginning to look that way.
One thing's for sure," he said, picking up the file and dropping it under Sean's nose again. "Connor doesn't have to
handle this case. You do."

"Why don't we shoot a game of pool and the loser takes
the case," Sean suggested.

"And let you hustle me again? No way."

"Then cards," Sean offered and bit off another chunk
of the chocolate. "Losing hand has to take the case."

"Forget it. And if you get food poisoning, don't think
that's going to get you off the hook."

As the rich chocolate melted in his mouth, Sean's reasoning processes began to clear. "How about Molly? I
heard she's considering taking a police officer's job in New
Orleans. Maybe she'd be interested in doing some PI work
here instead."

"Not a bad idea. I'll feel her out about it."

Sean polished off the rest of the candy bar, and when
Michael continued to claim the spot he'd taken up on the
corner of his desk, Sean asked, "Besides dumping more
work on me was there something else you wanted?"

"Actually, I wanted to talk to you about Katie."

Sean sobered instantly. "What about her?"

"I talked to Mom earlier. She wants us both to come to
dinner on Sunday," he said, removing a pencil from a cup
on the desk.

Sean snatched the pencil from his brother. "All right.

You want to tell me what Sunday dinner at home has to do with Katie?''

''While we were talking, Mom mentioned that according to Katie's mother Katie has been seeing someone, and it looks like things might be getting serious. Katie brought the guy to meet her mother this week.''

The pencil snapped in two as jealousy gripped Sean by the throat and refused to let go. Michael looked at the mangled pencil he was holding, then met his gaze.

''Just thought you'd want to know someone's trying to cut in on your territory. According to Mom, the fellow's been giving Katie the big rush. Expensive dinners, the ballet, theater. He even sent her mother flowers after meeting her.''

''This guy have a name?'' Sean asked, irritation and jealousy churning inside him.

''Scott is all Mom said.''

Scott Brennan, the stockbroker. Katie's third daddy candidate. Did she really think he'd let her go through with that fool plan of hers now?

''Mom just happened to be outside when he came over with Katie, and she met him.''

''Right,'' Sean replied, knowing darn good and well that there'd been nothing accidental about his mother checking out Brennan.

''According to Mom, the fellow's nice enough. Good-looking, and he seemed to be nuts about Katie.''

Sean shoved back from his desk and stood. ''Any more cheery news you want to share?''

''No. That's about it. You going somewhere?'' Michael asked as Sean headed for the door.

''Yeah. To talk some sense into Katie.''

"Uh, little brother, I have a suggestion."

Sean turned and looked at his brother. "What?"

"You might want to try doing something besides talking."

Nine

Sean pulled his Bronco up to the curb and parked behind a Toyota sporting matching baby seats in the back seat. Glancing at the clock on his dashboard that read 4:00 p.m., he cut off the engine and prepared to wait. This time he wasn't going to leave anything to chance, he promised himself. No more missing Katie at home. No more trading phone messages with her. The two of them were going to talk turkey, and they were going to do it now. Or at least as soon as he could kidnap her from work.

With his eyes trained on the door of the Three Bears Nursery School, Sean went over in his mind everything he wanted to tell Katie. No point in beating around the bush, he told himself. He would simply lay his cards out on the table, explain about the mess with Heather, and tell Katie flat-out that there was only one woman he was interested in—her—and that interest didn't fall under friendship.

As for Brennan, the guy could just take a hike, because

Sean had no intention of sharing Katie with him or any other man. The green-eyed monster reared its head again as he thought of Katie being kissed and touched by anyone other than him. The possessive feelings stirring inside him surprised him. Had he been kidding himself all these years that his protectiveness of Katie was rooted in friendship? Had the reason he'd found something wrong with every guy she'd dated been the result of his own deeper feelings for her? Sean smiled to himself as he mulled over that one. There was one thing he was sure about—he was going to enjoy exploring this new aspect of his relationship with Katie.

He was still musing over all the things he wanted to do to and with Katie when he suddenly became aware of the increased flow of traffic around him. Glancing at the clock again, he noted it was already past five. Anticipation hummed in his veins as he shifted his attention to the entrance of the nursery school. Women and men disappeared inside the bright red-and-yellow structure decorated with a string of nursery rhyme characters across the front. The doors opened and out came an obviously harried mother rushing behind a set of squealing twin boys who were running as fast as their tiny legs would take them. Three more women exited, all carrying children, but still no sign of Katie.

He trained his gaze on the doors like a hunter stalking its prey, and when they opened again he saw her. Katie. Excitement shot through him like a bullet as he drank in the sight of her. Dressed in a long, gypsy skirt of greens and golds, the fabric hugged her slim hips and flowed down her legs nearly to her ankles. A blouse the color of the antique gold locket that he'd often seen her wear was tucked into the waistband of her skirt. Scarves in the same shades of green and gold were wrapped snugly around her waist. She adjusted the straps of the huge gold bag hanging from one shoulder, then hoisted on her opposite hip a baby boy who seemed fascinated with the small gold hoops in her ears. A little girl of no more than four clung to one of Katie's legs, a fistful of the fanciful skirt wedged in her tiny fist.

Katie dipped her head to nuzzle the baby in her arms, and as she did so the afternoon sun caught her hair, glinting like a halo of red-gold. Laughing, she stooped down to brush a kiss to the cheek of the little girl. She looks like an angel, Sean thought, his chest tightening as he watched her with the children. Though she'd told him she wanted to have a baby, and he'd always known Katie loved kids, until now he'd never really pictured her as a mother. Now he could all too easily envision Katie pregnant, her belly swollen with child, another baby nursing at her breast. His child, Sean amended, then nearly choked at how strongly the idea appealed to him. That he would even think such a thing shook him. Intrigued him. Scared the pants off him.

One step at a time, Sean told himself as he watched Katie kiss the baby goodbye and hand him over to his mother. When she hugged the little girl and started to hand her off, Sean exited the Bronco and started down the sidewalk toward her.

He knew the moment she spotted him. Her body stilled, and despite the smile she'd pasted on her lips, he didn't miss the slight tremor of her fingers before she folded her arms and tucked her hands out of sight. He didn't blame her for being nervous, Sean told himself. So much had been left hanging between them after that night in the storm, and his trip out of town had only added to the tension. But the wariness in her expression disturbed him, ripped at him like a knife. He wanted Katie to desire him as he did her, to want him so much she couldn't see straight. Maybe a part of him even wanted her to fall in love with him—at least a little. What he didn't want, what shamed him, was the notion that he had given her reason to fear him.

"Sean, what a surprise," she said as he drew closer.

Capturing her hands in his, he dipped his head and brushed his lips gently across hers, when what he really wanted to do was drag her into his arms and feast on her mouth until they were both trembling. Heat already racing in his blood, he forced himself to end the kiss. "Hi, stranger."

She looked at him as though she were having trouble focusing for a moment, then she took a step back. "What on earth are you doing here?"

"Waiting for you."

She blinked. "Why? Is something wrong?"

"Yeah," he told her, closing the distance between them again. He ran a finger across the little crease forming between her brows and once again he felt that tightening, that swelling in his chest. "I've missed you, Malloy. And I haven't had a decent night's sleep in more than a week because I can't stop thinking about you."

She opened her mouth, then closed it.

Sean chuckled. "I don't believe it. This has got to be a first. Katie Malloy speechless."

The remark had the desired effect because her eyes cleared, cooled. Straightening her spine, she tipped up her chin. "With compliments like that one, Fitzpatrick, it sure beats me how you got such a reputation as a ladies' man."

Sean winked at her. "I don't think it was my way with compliments that had anything to do with it. But I'll be happy to demonstrate what did."

Ignoring his suggestive remark, she asked, "So, when did you get back?"

"This morning."

"One of the messages you left on my machine said you had a lead on Connor. Any luck?"

"No," Sean admitted, still disappointed by that fact. "But I didn't come here to talk about Connor, or to play Twenty Questions with you."

"Twenty Questions?"

"Yeah. You know, that little trick of yours where you ask me about work and family and remind me what good friends we are so you can distract me? Well, it isn't going to work this time."

She looked at him as though he was insane. And perhaps he was, Sean told himself, but he was through dancing around the fact that there was a heck of a lot more going on between them than friendship.

"I don't know what's gotten into you. I was just trying to be polite. As for our being friends, that's what I thought we were. But maybe I was mistaken, because no friend—"

Sean snagged her hand and tugged her closer. "Don't. I'm tired of us both trying to shove what's happening between us under some rug and labeling it friendship. I am not here because I'm your friend, Katie."

"Then why are you here?"

"Because I want you," he said, sliding his hand behind her neck and forcing her to look at him. "You're all I've been able to think about for weeks. I can't eat. I can't sleep. I can barely think for wanting you."

Katie swallowed. "Sean, I—"

"I want to make love with you," he told her, his voice hard, just short of violent. "I want you naked and hot beneath me—in my bed, your bed, on that couch in your den, on the deck under the stars. I want you anywhere. Everywhere. I want to finish what we started that night in the rainstorm, and this time I don't want to stop until I'm buried inside you so deep that you're screaming my name. And I want it to be my name you scream, Katie. Mine.''

She trembled. Her eyes darkened. Unable to resist, Sean eased his grip to slide his fingers to the pulse beating wildly in her throat. The need in him twisted a notch tighter. "And if you keep looking at me like that," he practically growled the warning as desire burned inside him, "we may not even make it to my truck.''

"Miss Katie. Miss Katie,'' a child's impatient voice worked its way through his desire-fogged senses.

Katie jerked her gaze from his to stare down at the little girl tugging on her skirt. She swallowed, took a step back, pulling free of his hold. "Yes, Lisa?" she asked, her voice cracking. She swallowed again. "What is it, sweetie?''

Drawing a deep breath, Sean reined in his nearly out-of-control emotions and took note of his surroundings. Cars lined both sides of the street now, two blocks deep in either direction. Kids and adults marched up and down the sidewalk to and from the school like ants. Yet he'd been so caught up in Katie, in the heat wrapping around them, that he hadn't even noticed. For a man who once considered himself to possess a fair amount of finesse with women, he hadn't exhibited an ounce of it just now, he admitted. The sidewalk of a nursery school was not the appropriate place to tell a woman that he wanted to make love with her. Sean scrubbed a hand down his face, wondering how the woman managed to drive him straight to flashpoint with nothing more than a look.

"Mommy said I could come tell you 'bye." The little girl gave Katie a loud-sounding smack to the cheek. "I love you.''

"And I love you, too, sweetie." Smiling, Katie hugged the brown-eyed moppet close for a moment, and Sean could have sworn he saw tears shimmering in her eyes. "I'll see you on Monday, okay?"

"'Kay," Lisa said, waving goodbye.

After a moment, when Katie didn't move but simply stared after the child, Sean offered her his hand, resisted the urge to gather her into his arms. He still wanted to make love to her, to learn all the secrets of her body and to teach her his. But he also wanted to soothe away the wistfulness that he'd sensed when she held the little girl. Most of all, he just wanted to be alone with Katie. "You ready to go?" he asked, and started to guide her to his truck.

She came to a halt. "What about my car? I can't leave my car here."

"Fine. We'll take your car, and I'll leave my truck. Where are you parked, around back?" He didn't wait for her to answer, simply started for the lot he'd spied in the rear of the building.

"But what about your truck?"

"You can bring me back to pick it up later."

They made it to the parking lot when she dug in her heels a second time. "I can't do this, Sean. I can't just hop into bed with you."

"Katie," he murmured, drawing her to him.

"No," she repeated, pushing away from him. "I can't think when you're touching me," she told him, which brought a smile to his lips and to his soul. "You're moving too fast for me."

His smile died a swift death. "Considering the fact that it's taken us almost twenty years to get this far, I don't think we're setting any records for speed here."

Her eyes snapped with temper. "You know what I mean. Until recently you barely gave me a second look. And you certainly haven't been trying to hustle me into bed for the past twenty years."

He'd tell her later that he had given her second and third and fourth and more looks over the years, but fear of losing her friendship had made him keep her at arm's length. It was only recently that he'd realized some thing's were worth the risk. Instead he said, "Obviously I was an idiot."

"On that we agree."

He ignored the dig. "We want each other, Katie, and I for one am tired of making excuses why we shouldn't do something about it." He paused, realizing how irritated he sounded, and how hard he was pushing her. "Or am I wrong in thinking you feel the same way? That you want me, too? If I am, tell me now."

"You're not wrong," she said, her voice little more than a whisper. "I do want you."

"Ah, sweetheart," Sean said, reaching for her.

"Don't." She put up a hand to ward him off. "I told you I can't think straight when you touch me."

Biting back a chuckle, Sean tucked his hands in his pockets, and decided it best not to comment on that one. "So why are we still standing here? Haven't we wasted enough time figuring out how we feel about each other?"

"And how do you feel about me, Sean? I need to know."

Quicksand would have proven sturdier under his feet than the concrete parking lot, he thought, as he stared into Katie's sweet, vulnerable face. He'd told other women he'd loved them and meant it at the time, but no one had ever been as important to him as Katie. Somehow the words *I love you* didn't seem big enough for what she meant to him. Brushing her cheek with his thumb, he said, "I feel alive when I'm with you, half-dead when we're apart. You complete me in a way no one else ever has."

Her eyes clouded, brimmed with tears, then she threw her arms around him and gave him a slap-dash kiss. "I love you," she told him. "Take your truck. I'll take my car and meet you at home."

Sean had no chance to object because she spun around and raced over to her Jeep, and then the little green CJ7 was pulling out of the lot past him. Grinning like a love-happy sap, he ran back out to the street to his Bronco. Determined to beat her home and ice that bottle of champagne he'd been saving, Sean started up his truck's engine and threw it into gear.

He pulled up to the curb in front of the apartment complex just as Katie turned the corner. Still smiling he jumped out of the Bronco and headed for the stairs. He was so busy monitoring Katie's progress that he didn't even see the brunette until she'd launched herself at him and planted her lips on his. Grabbing the arms wrapped around his neck, Sean stared into the face of the gorgeous brunette dressed in a navy-blue airline uniform that molded centerfold curves.

"Sean, honey, I had a layover in Chicago and decided to take you up on your offer."

Panic shot through him like a rocket as Katie marched up the steps. "Don't mind me," she said, her voice cool, her eyes downright frigid as she walked past them. "I'll be out of your way in just a second, and then you can go back to…to whatever it is you were doing."

Sean swore. "Katie, wait!"

And the quiet click of her apartment door closing was ten times more deafening than if she had slammed it.

"Her name's Melody," Sean told Katie two hours later as he followed her through her apartment and into the bedroom. "I met her on a flight about a year ago, and we…well, it's been over a long time."

Katie looked at his scowling image in her dressing table

mirror as she dabbed perfume behind her ears, her wrists, the back of her knees. Oh, it had taken every ounce of pride in her to march past him and that sultry-mouthed brunette without grabbing the woman and ripping her out of Sean's arms. But she'd done it. She'd used that same stubborn pride to keep the tears at bay while she'd accepted Scott's invitation to dinner, showered and changed. And it was pride, again, that had made her finally open the door and let Sean into her apartment. What amazed her, though, was that she could face him now with the semblance of calm detachment while her heart felt so battered and bruised.

"I wasn't expecting her. She had a layover and decided to drop by."

"I've already told you that you don't owe me any explanations," she said, drawing the top of the crystal perfume bottle down her throat to the vee of her dress.

"I know that," he snapped and raked a hand through his hair. "I was just stating the facts so you'd understand."

Katie arched a brow as she met his eyes in the mirror. "Oh, I understand," she said as she fastened the diamond teardrops in her ears.

"You do?" he asked, his expression as skeptical as his voice.

"Sure." The doorbell rang, and she stood. Picking up the little black evening bag, she turned around to face him. "And I also understand that what you do and who you do it with really isn't any of my business. Now, if you'll excuse me, I believe that's my date."

"Your date?"

"That's right." Sweeping past the furious-eyed man should have been balm to her wounded heart. When he'd sworn a blue streak, darted after her and insisted on meeting Scott, whom he'd treated like someone on the post office's ten-most-wanted list, it should have at the very least given her a smidgen of satisfaction. But it didn't. And despite Scott's understanding ear and attempts to lighten her mood, that achy feeling in her heart, that emptiness that it seemed only Sean could fill, had grown even more painful by the next evening.

"Earth to Katie."

Katie dragged her thoughts back to the man seated across from her. "I beg your pardon?"

"No need to beg," Scott said, a smile curving his handsome face, his brown eyes twinkling. He bent toward her and whispered, "But were I a lesser man, the fact that you haven't heard a thing I've said to you in the past ten minutes would be murder on my ego."

"I'm sorry, Scott," Katie said, guilt heating her cheeks as she glanced across the table at him. "It's not you."

He chuckled. "I know, but don't expect me to let you off the hook so easily. You do realize that I was well on my way to falling in love with you. Then I realized that you didn't feel the same way about me."

"I'm sorry," she told him again. And she was. She was also the world's biggest fool, Katie told herself not for the first time. Scott was wonderful. He was everything any woman could want—charming, attentive, fun to be with. He was perfect—except for the simple fact that he wasn't Sean. And it was Sean that she loved.

"So am I. I still can't figure out how a smart woman like you could actually prefer a guy like Fitzpatrick over an ideal specimen like me," he told her jokingly.

"That makes two of us," she replied, grateful to him for easing her guilt. "But I guess our hearts don't always agree with what our heads tell us. Someone once said that love chooses us and not the other way around. I guess they were right."

Scott reached for her hand, squeezed her fingers. "You sure he doesn't feel the same way about you?"

"I know he cares about me, even wants me. But caring about someone, wanting them physically, it isn't the same thing as love."

"It's possible he'll grow to love you."

"He might. But I don't want him to have to learn to love me or to feel obligated to love me because I love him. Love should be so big, so huge and overwhelming that you don't have any choice in how you feel. It just takes hold of you and doesn't let go. That's how I feel about Sean."

"Sounds like a nasty case of the flu to me," Scott teased. "Maybe the right man, given a chance, would help you forget him."

His offer touched her deeply. "Thank you, but I'm afraid it isn't quite that simple. There isn't any magic cure for loving someone who doesn't love you. I'm just going to have to learn to live with it." She'd come to that conclusion during the long, sleepless night.

"Anything I can do to help?"

Katie thought of her plans for a baby, and admitted that there would be no babies for her. Mrs. Fitzpatrick had been right after all, although she'd known it for some time now. Having a baby should be the fruit of two people's love, and the man she loved, the only man she would ever love, was Sean. "You've already done plenty just by listening. But would you mind terribly if we cut the evening short. I'm not really in the mood for the theater tonight." And she knew she needed to sit down and talk to Sean if she was going to try to salvage their friendship. There was no point in putting it off any longer.

"No problem," he said, and signaled the waiter for their check.

Thirty minutes later Scott held open the door for her, and

she exited the sleek, silver sports car. "I'm sorry I wasn't better company tonight."

"You're always good company, Katie, even when you're mooning over the wrong guy."

She laughed. "I don't know what I would have done without you these past few days," she told him as he walked her to her front door.

"Anytime," he said, and brushed a friendly kiss across her mouth. "I mean that. And if you come to your senses and decide I'm too good to pass up, you just pick up the phone and call me."

"You're a sweetheart," she told him, patting his cheek. "Some lucky girl's going to scoop you up fast."

"Does that mean you've had a change of heart?" Propping one arm up over her door, he looked down at her with a teasing light in his eyes. "I hope so because I was already picking out china and crystal and names for our kids."

Katie laughed. "China patterns and kids, huh?" she replied as she removed her key from her evening bag to unlock her door.

"Yep." He wiggled his dark brows in exaggeration. "I figure at our advanced ages we'd have to get busy fast if we were going to produce a half-dozen little Brennans the way my folks did."

"You want six kids?"

"You bet."

"Then you'd better find yourself another woman, pal," Sean told him, his voice deadly, his eyes even more lethal.

"Sean, don't," Katie called out.

He ignored her. Grabbing Scott by the back of his jacket, Sean pulled him away from her, and shoved him up against the wall. "Consider this an addendum to that report I gave you earlier, Ms. Malloy. Brennan here already has a fiancée."

"What?" Scott shook free of Sean's hold and glaring at him, he smoothed out his jacket. "I don't know what you're drinking, pal, but I am definitely not engaged."

"No? Does the name Laura Baker ring any bells?"

Confused, Katie's gaze swiveled from Sean to Scott's.

"Laura Baker," Scott repeated, the lines on his forehead drawing into a frown. "The only Laura Baker I know is a girl I dated in high school."

"One and the same," Sean informed him. "Do you remember giving her your class ring when you were a senior in high school, and asking her to marry you when you finished college?"

"You're kidding," Scott replied, astonishment written all over his face. "That was more than fifteen years ago. I was just a kid."

"You were eighteen, an adult, and you never broke off the engagement or asked for the ring back."

"So?"

"So since she's still single, technically, you and Laura are still engaged."

"You're nuts," Scott told him.

"No, you are, if you think I'm going to let you try to get Katie pregnant when you're already engaged to someone else."

"Get her preg—" Shock registered on Scott's face. "This is crazy."

It was crazy. But it was also the act of a desperate man, Katie realized, and her heart practically sang with joy. Sean, the lovable idiot, didn't realize that she could never have gone through with her baby plans, that she'd abandoned them some time ago when she realized it was Sean that she loved.

"The only one who's crazy is you, pal, if you think I'll let you anywhere near Katie." He yanked open the door of the apartment building that led from the entryway to the street.

Not the least bit intimidated by Sean, Scott jerked free. He shot his gaze to her. "Katie?"

"It's okay, Scott. You'd better go. Obviously Sean and I need to talk," she told him.

"If you're sure."

She nodded.

"I'll call you later to make sure you're all right," Scott said. After tossing a glare at Sean, he left.

Nervous anticipation bubbled through her as Katie turned her back to Sean and entered her apartment.

Sean followed her inside. "I suppose you're ticked off at me again."

"Don't you think I have reason?" Dropping her purse on the table, she slipped off the evening jacket to the strapless black dress she wore.

"I think you should be grateful," he told her, an edge in his voice.

"Not likely," she said, and headed for the kitchen, where she removed the pitcher of iced tea from the refrigerator. When she turned, he was standing in the doorway. "Want some?"

"No."

She shrugged. Retrieving a glass from the cabinet, she poured herself some tea and returned the pitcher to the refrigerator. "You had no right to treat Scott that way. You're not my keeper, Sean."

"Yeah, well, maybe you need a keeper."

Something in his tone gave her pause. She noted the dangerous gleam in his eyes. She started to take a step back, then caught herself. "And I suppose you're offering to fill the position?" she taunted, despite the butterflies jumping in her stomach.

"What if I am?" he replied, his expression as hard as his voice.

Refusing to be intimidated, she hiked up her chin and met his furious gaze. With an aplomb in direct opposition to the nerves twisting inside her, Katie patted his cheek. "No thanks. I think I'll just keep you as a friend."

"That's it," he snapped, and in the blink of an eye he was in her face. "You just had to toss that word *friend* at me again, didn't you?"

Katie took a step back and met the refrigerator. "Sean—"

He caught her by the shoulders, jerked her against him and took possession of her mouth. The glass in her hand tumbled to the floor, shattered, as he plundered her lips. His hands raced over her, cupped her bottom and pulled her to him. He tore his mouth free long enough to say, "I'm through playing games with you, Katie Malloy, and I'm tired of you using the word *friend* like some kind of shield against me."

Then he attacked her mouth again, making her head spin, leaving her breathless and quivering as his impatient lips, his hot, urgent hands sent heat and need pouring through her.

"I don't want to be your damn friend," he snapped between kisses. "I want to be your lover," he told her, dipping for another taste, another touch. "You got that?"

"I— Yes. No." How could she think when her legs had turned to jelly and her brain was melting faster than butter on hot bread? His fingers worked at the back of her dress. She felt it fall to her feet. Then his mouth closed over the tip of her breast. Katie moaned. When he moved to taste her other breast, she tore at the buttons of his shirt, ran her fingers over his muscles, through the hair on his chest, over his racing heart, down his tight belly, then lower still, searching for the source of his heat. Finding it, she stroked his hardened length.

He groaned, swore. Lifting her up into his arms, he marched out of the kitchen, pausing en route to her bedroom for another quick taste, another drugging kiss, another reassuring touch.

"I— Sean, we need to think about what we're doing. We need to talk," she told him, panic and need warring inside her when he set her down on her feet beside the bed.

"To hell with thinking and talking. What I need...all I need is you." He clenched his hands at his sides, fury and frustration etched in every line of his beautiful face, in his magnificent body. He drew a ragged breath. "Do you want me to stop?"

And he would stop, Katie realized. Despite the fact that they were both near fever pitch, he would stop now if she asked him to. But she didn't ask him to stop. She didn't want to think. She didn't want to talk. What she needed, what she wanted was to make love with him. "No," she told him, and reached for the snap on his jeans. "I don't want you to stop. I want you to hurry."

She didn't have to tell him twice. Swooping down to capture her mouth again, Sean hurried. So did she. Somehow those clever, urgent fingers of his had her naked in seconds and tumbled onto the bed.

Before her vision could clear, his mouth was on hers again, feasting with tongue and teeth and lips, firing arrows of liquid heat to her center and making her dizzy with need. Hot, callused hands swept over her breasts, down her hips, between her thighs, sending wave after wave of sensation screaming through her.

She'd never been in a hurricane before, but she was sure no hurricane could possibly match this heat, this speed, this urgency of Sean's mouth, of Sean's hands on her flesh.

Surely no hurricane could match the powerful storm of
need ripping through her to have Sean inside her.

"Aw, hell," Sean muttered and pulled away to kick off
his shoes, shed his pants.

She dragged away the shirt still covering his back and
pressed her mouth against his bare shoulders, licked his hot
flesh with her tongue.

Sean swore again, his fingers fumbling with the latex
sheath as he rolled on protection. Whipping around, he
tumbled her back against the sheets and moved over her.
Desire burned in his eyes, turning them nearly black, and
knowing that he wanted her so fiercely sent new arrows of
heat firing through Katie, sharpening her own need, her
own urgency. "Oh hurry. Hurry," Katie pleaded, reaching
for his hips. "I don't want to wait any longer. I can't wait
any longer," she amended. "I want you inside me. Now."

He made a strangled sound, part curse, part groan, and
then he drove himself in her in one hard stroke. Katie
arched her back instinctively and took him in deeper. He
swore again. Sweat broke out across his brow, dampened
his back. She wanted to watch him take her, fill her, make
them one. She opened her mouth to tell him, but his tongue
dove between her lips to mate. She tasted frustration in his
kiss, impatient need, yearning. A yearning so sweet, so
huge, it made her heart leap in her breast with hope, with
love.

But then he slammed into her again, flesh to flesh, hip
to hip, driving deep, deep, deeper still, stealing her breath,
scattering all thoughts except the frenzied need to join her
body with his. She locked her legs around his waist, and
when she lifted her hips, rushed up to meet his urgent
thrusts, the hurricane broke free inside her. She clung to
him and, crying out his name, she went hurdling heart and
body and soul into the eye of the storm.

Ten

She shuddered beneath him—quick, fierce shudders that confirmed his fears that he'd hurt her. In losing control he'd been too rough with her, just short of brutal, and it shamed him to know that he had caused her pain. He'd made love before, enough times to know what a roller-coaster ride it sometimes could be. But nothing, nothing he'd experienced before had prepared him for making love with Katie. She'd flat-out destroyed him—not only with her warm, welcoming body, but with her sweet demands, with those sexy, little moans she made deep in her throat. One look at the wonderment in her eyes, the sheer pleasure on her face as he entered her, and he'd lost the last threads of control. The beast in him had broken free, and the need to claim her, to make her his, had consumed him. He'd taken her hard and fast. Too hard and too fast.

Levering himself up on his elbows, he looked down at her, and winced at the sweep of whisker burns that stood out like accusing fingers against the pale creamy skin on her face and breasts. Guilt gnawed at him, damned him for not taking more care. "You okay?"

Her eyes fluttered, opened, and as she stared up at him a smile curved her lips. "Oh, I think I'm a lot better than okay. I feel wonderful." She all but purred and stretched her body like a contented cat, nearly scrambling his brain a second time when her feminine muscles tightened around him.

Desire punched through him again, and Sean rolled off onto his back so as not to give in to temptation and take them both flying again. "I, uh, I was worried I hurt you. I got a little rough. Hell." He took a deep breath and washed a hand down his face. "I got a lot rough, and I rushed things. I shouldn't have."

"I seem to recall being in a bit of a hurry myself," she informed him, laughter in her voice.

"Yeah, you were." Sean smiled at that and began to relax. Katie had definitely been as hot and eager for him as he had been for her, and she hadn't been at all shy about letting him know she wanted him. Reaching for her, he settled her in the crook of his arms to cuddle, enjoying her warmth, her closeness. He brushed a lock of hair back from her face and traced his fingers down her cheek. She was so soft. He couldn't remember any other woman who had skin this soft, who had eyes that exact shade of brandy, who had a mouth that could make him beg to taste or who had felt so good, so right, in his arms. His chest swelled, almost hurt, at just how good, how right it felt to be lying with her like this. And he could see them lying here together like this for a long, long time.

"You're an incredible lover," she murmured, capturing one of his hands and nuzzling his palm. She kissed his fingers, flicked them with her tongue, and desire sparked,

licked low in his belly when he didn't think it was physically possible. "It...making love, has never been like that
for me before. It's never been so...so powerful."

"Same here," he admitted. Making love with her had
been a mind-blowing experience. Maybe it was because he
knew Katie so well, was so comfortable with her outside
of bed, he told himself. Yet, being with her like this was
all so new, so exciting, and so right.

As she continued to make love to his fingers with her
mouth, her other hand drifted down his chest, over his
stomach, lower. "You have such a beautiful body, Sean,"
she whispered, and closed her fingers around him.

The air backed up in his lungs. His vision blurred.
"Sweet heaven, Katie," he hissed. He gulped in air and
tried to concentrate on forcing it in and out of his lungs.
"I need time to recover."

Raising herself up on one elbow, she looked down at
him. And those brown eyes of hers were pure sin as she
asked, "How much time?"

"Not a lot," he told her, the heat already flashing hotter,
higher, faster. She nipped his shoulder with sharp teeth,
making him gasp. Then she followed the bite with the wash
of her tongue.

She pushed herself up to her knees, and with a sinful
smile to match those eyes, she straddled his hips and said,
"You just let me know when you've recovered." And she
proceeded to press hot, wet kisses to his chest while she
rubbed that long, narrow body of hers against him. Her
teeth scraped across his nipple, and he nearly came apart.

Sean flipped her onto her back. "I'm all recovered," he
informed her and launched his own assault on her mouth.

When he lifted his head to drag in air, she smiled at him
again. "You recover fast, Fitzpatrick."

"It's the Irish genes," he murmured, and reached for the packet on the bedside table.

She took it from him, ripped the packet open with her teeth. "I knew there was a reason I've always been fond of the Irish," she whispered huskily as she smoothed the condom over him. He shuddered beneath the feel of her fingers on him. "You Irish have such remarkable genes."

"Katie, love, you have no idea just how remarkable this Irishman can be."

"Why don't you show me," she challenged.

And he did show her. Over and over and over again.

Damn, but life was good, Sean decided. Leaning back in the chair at his desk, he smiled as his thoughts drifted to Katie. They had been lovers for nearly a month now, and despite any initial fears either of them had had about the effects their new intimacy would have on their friendship, things were just fine. In fact, if it were possible, things seemed to get better and better.

He still couldn't believe his luck. Even knowing Katie as well as he did, he'd never dreamed he could enjoy anyone this much, or want any woman this much. But he did enjoy her, and he wanted her more all the time. He especially liked waking up with her. Images of this morning flashed into his mind's eye—Katie with her leg draped over his, her head snuggled against his chest. Even after last night's lovemaking, he'd awakened this morning hot, ready and wanting her again. She'd looked so soft and sexy lying there wearing nothing but his shirt. He'd been unable to resist running his hand up that long, smooth leg and slipping his fingers beneath the shirt to touch her breasts.

"Mmm," she mumbled, curling against him like a contented cat. "Don't stop."

He didn't. He'd made love to her again, and it had been

as slow and tender as last night's coming together had been fast and untamed. Later when she'd joined him in the shower, and they'd soaped each other's bodies and made love until the water ran cold, he'd been positive that he could get through the day without wanting her again.

He'd been wrong, Sean admitted, the blood in his veins already heating. Maybe he could call Katie at the nursery, and ask if she could leave work early.

"What in the hell are you smiling about?"

Sean blinked. He swallowed his smile and reluctantly shoved his plans for an early evening with Katie on the back burner. Staring at Michael, he noted the scowl on his brother's face. "Just thinking ahead to this evening," Sean informed him, eyeing with suspicion the armload of files Michael was holding.

"Well, whatever you've got planned, cancel it. You'll be working late. You just inherited a new batch of clients."

"The hell I did! Hold on a damn minute," Sean protested, as Michael dumped the mess of folders on top of his desk. Furious, Sean jumped to his feet, fists ready, and had to check the urge to fly at his brother. "Forget it. No way am I taking on any more cases. My plate's already too full."

"Then it just got a little fuller."

"No. I mean it, Michael. I'm not doing it. You need somebody to work those cases," he replied, motioning to the sliding stack of expando folders, "then give them to Ryan."

"These are Ryan's," Michael advised him. Then he sank to the chair in front of him and rubbed a hand over the back of his neck. Michael sighed. "The man's not worth spit with Clea due anyday now. I sent him home. I had to. I know this is their first baby and that Clea's had some complications, but it's embarrassing to watch the guy. He jumps and gets this look of terror in his eyes, every time the phone rings.''

Sean tried to imagine how he would feel if it were Katie pregnant with his child. Surprisingly he found the idea appealing. The fact that he did had a knot twisting in his gut.

''Anyway, I just couldn't take it anymore. Besides I was worried Tracy would up and quit if he asked her one more time if she was sure the phones were working and that Clea hadn't called for him.''

''He's nervous,'' Sean reasoned.

''You think I don't know that?'' Michael shoved out of the chair and began pacing in front of Sean's desk. ''But between Ryan climbing the walls waiting for Clea to have their baby and you walking around here like a lovesick puppy mooning over some female—''

''I haven't been mooning over any female,'' Sean protested, irritated by the accusation.

''Right,'' Michael shot back with a snicker. ''And what were you doing when I came in here just now and found you with that sappy grin on your face? You going to tell me you weren't hip-deep in thought about some woman?''

He couldn't. Because it wouldn't be true. He had been wrapped up in thoughts of Katie. But no way was he about to admit that to Michael. ''I told you, I was thinking about my plans for the evening.''

''Which have to be canceled,'' Michael repeated, pausing in front of Sean's desk. He leaned forward, got that courtroom lawyer look on his face. ''I mean it, Sean. We've got a business to run here, and our clients have expectations, demands that have to be met. Somebody has to give them the service they're paying for, and since Ryan is going to be useless until that baby gets here, you're elected. So these are all yours.''

''The hell they are!'' He'd been working like a madman

for weeks now, clearing off his desk, closing out as many cases as he could, so that he could shave off a few days for a long weekend away with Katie. He was just beginning to think he might be able to pull it off, but taking on any new cases would deep-six that plan for sure. "I'm already carrying more than my share since I took over Ryan's out-of-town cases."

"You took half of them. I took the rest," Michael reminded him. "But if it's any consolation, these are local. There's not an overnighter in the bunch," Michael informed him, and started for the door.

"Damn it, Michael. Get your carcass back in here, or so help me, I'm going to stuff that fifty-dollar tie of yours down your throat."

"It cost seventy-five bucks, not fifty, and you're welcome to try," Michael told him with a snarl, but he retraced his steps. For the first time Sean noted the weariness in his brother's face, the concern in his eyes. Guilt licked at Sean, and he admitted to himself that he hadn't worried about the agency or the backlog of clients overmuch because he'd relied on Michael to see that everything ran smoothly. And despite the extra hours he'd been putting in so that he could go off for some fun with Katie, he knew Michael put in just as many hours with little complaint. "All right. I'll take half of them, but you're taking the other half."

"Done."

The easy agreement hit Sean like a sucker punch. "You weasel," Sean snapped, realizing at once that he'd been had. "You only wanted me to take half to begin with."

Michael grinned and began dividing the folders. "It's called psychology, little brother, and it works on you every time."

"Funny. Maybe you should have become a shrink instead of a detective,'' Sean muttered, sorting through the files Michael was divvying into two stacks.

''So, who is she?'' Michael asked, his mood noticeably lighter now that he had tricked him into taking on the extra work.

Sean hesitated. It wasn't that he was embarrassed to admit that it was Katie he was seeing. Far from it. But so far, Katie hadn't given any indication that she wanted their families or friends to know about the change in their relationship. In fact, now that he thought about it, he realized that they never went out like normal couples did. She seemed to prefer eating in and renting a video, just spending time together without the courting rituals. He hadn't objected because it had made things simpler. When desire struck, which it invariably did with frequency, there had been no rush to get home or excuses to make. Clothes disappeared. Mouth came to mouth, flesh to flesh. The couch, the kitchen floor, that big chair in her den worked as well as any bed and made for interesting positions and exciting climaxes. And with Katie there had been plenty of both—more than he'd ever dreamed possible. Certainly more than he'd ever shared with anyone else.

''Well, I'll be damned.''

Sean jerked his attention back to Michael who sat across from him, a thick file in his hand and an eyebrow arched in speculation. ''What?''

Michael chuckled. ''From the expression on your face, I'm actually beginning to think you might be serious about the woman.''

''I'm always serious about women.''

''Uh-huh. So who is she? And when do I get to meet her?''

''You've already met her. It's Katie.''

"Our Katie? Katie Malloy?" Michael asked, then threw his head back and started to laugh.

"My Katie," Sean corrected, surprising himself with his need to stake a claim. It was only because Michael had dated her, Sean reasoned. Annoyed that his brother found the idea of him with Katie so amusing, Sean grumbled, "As soon as you finish your imitation of a hyena, why don't you let me in on the joke?"

"You are the joke, Bro," Michael said, wiping tears from his eyes. "I mean I knew sooner or later a woman was going to come along and take you down, if for no other reason than the fact that you were so sure no woman could. But I swear I never dreamed that woman would turn out to be Katie."

"You don't know what you're talking about." Sweat broke out across his brow. His palms grew damp. "Nobody's taking me down."

"Want to bet? Face it, little brother, your bachelor days are about to come to an end."

"You better check to see what's in that coffee you've been drinking, Bro. Ryan's married, and you're the one who's been making noises about settling down. Not me." But if he did, would Katie take him? He wasn't even close to being any fairy-tale Prince Charming, and he knew it. The last thing, the very last thing, he wanted to do was disappoint her the way her father and the other men in her life had done.

"Yeah, but I'm not the one with all the symptoms. You are."

"What symptoms?"

"The same ones Ryan had just before he took the fall. That goofy, dazed look in the eyes like the one you have now. The thoughts drifting off a hundred times a day the way you've been doing lately. And my guess is it would be a pretty safe bet to say you haven't even noticed another woman or even wanted one since you've been with Katie. Have you?"

He hadn't, he admitted, a sinking sensation sweeping through him at the realization. And every blasted word Michael had said was true.

"Take my word for it. You're done, pal. Might as well stick a fork in you because you're in love with Katie."

"You don't know what you're talking about," Sean countered, afraid to even think it was true. He'd never been in love—not the way Michael meant—and he didn't want to fall in love with a woman he didn't have a prayer of making happy.

"No?"

"No," Sean assured him.

"Must have read you wrong, then."

"Damn right you did."

"So you're just using Katie for sex."

Sean came at him, grabbed him by his fancy tie. "I am not! Damn it, I care about her!" The way he'd never cared about anyone before. Releasing his hold on Michael, he dropped back down to his seat and grabbed his head in his hands. "Aw, hell. I am in love with her, and I think I'm going to be sick."

"Lean your head down," Michael told him while he smoothed out his tie. "What about Katie? How does she feel?"

Sean battled back the sick feeling in his stomach and lifted his head. He didn't have a clue, which made him feel ten times worse. Sure she'd told him she loved him once. But that was before they'd become lovers, and she'd never said it again. He knew they were good together in bed and enjoyed each other out of it. But he honestly didn't know how she felt about him. Annoyed, scared, he shot back, "How do I know how she feels? I never asked her."

Michael shook his head, gave him a pitying look. "You don't have to ask, pal. Women let you know. It's their nature."

"Well, it's not Katie's nature. She's different."

"She never told you she loved you? Not even when you were tangled in the sheets?"

Katie hadn't told him she loved him again. But she couldn't have given herself to him as she had so completely, without her heart being involved. So why had she never again told him she loved him?

"She dropping any hints about getting married or the two of you moving in together?"

"No." Not a one. And damn it, why hadn't she? In his experience, all women wanted some sort of commitment or to at least know where the relationship was going. But Katie hadn't asked him. Not once. Not a word.

Michael rubbed his jaw. "She been leaving stuff over at your place? You know, clothes, girl stuff? Sort of moving in?"

"Not so much as a toothbrush," Sean told him, despite the fact that he'd told her she should. But she hadn't. Oh, she'd given him plausible excuses—she lived right next door, she wouldn't remember where her things were. But that's what they were—excuses to cover her reluctance to leave a part of herself with him. Well, she was too late, because she'd already left her mark. He'd gotten used to having her there, to being with her. Even when she wasn't there, he could still smell her on his sheets, in his bathroom, in her disastrous efforts in his kitchen. And now that he thought about it, she had never even mentioned anything about having a baby again.

Michael came around the desk and slapped a hand on

his shoulder. ''You've got a real problem, little brother. Katie's a smart girl. Evidently she's too smart to fall for the likes of you. If I were you I'd forget her and find someone else.''

''The hell I will,'' Sean told him. Pushing his brother aside, he stormed out of the office. Maybe he was no Prince Charming, but nobody knew Katie the way he did. Nobody knew all the little things that made her so special. Nobody knew that she liked old movies, melting ice cream and her steak burned. That she loved rainstorms, flowers and snowball fights. That she was a sucker for little kids and animals. That she had a smile that could light up a room and warm the coldest of days. That she had a heart as big as the sky. No, nobody knew Katie the way he did, and nobody could love her the way he did. And he'd be damned if he was going to give her up without a fight. She wanted Prince Charming? Then he'd be Prince Charming. Or he'd die trying.

Katie entered her apartment and stared at the flowers again. Roses. Beautiful, long-stemmed, red roses. A dozen of them sent that very morning from Sean. And just looking at them made her want to weep. She walked past the sweet-smelling bouquet, and that sick, sick feeling that she'd been trying to ignore all week hit her again. She was about to be dumped.

Dropping her bag to the table, she sank down onto the couch and leaned her head back against the cushion. Sadness settled over her like a shroud, zapping her already-diminished energy.

Time to face the truth, Katie girl. No use pretending you don't know. Because she did know. The flowers this morning had only been the clincher—the classic peace offering for guilt. She had to face the facts. Sean wanted to end their affair.

All the signs were there, she acknowledged, and had been for nearly a week. She just hadn't wanted to believe it. Still didn't, if she were honest with herself. But she had no choice. After more than a month of wonderful, exciting evenings and weekends spent in each other's company, the sudden dinners out in fancy restaurants, the movies at the theater and the opening-night seats for a new play in town two nights ago, had been the first signals that something was wrong. Sean's insistence that he take her dancing at some swanky club last night, when she knew darn well that the man didn't like to dance, had only been added proof that things were about to change. Oh, he'd been a perfect gentleman, a real prince of a guy.

Only she didn't want any fairy-tale prince. She wanted Sean. The Sean who was comfortable with her, who teased her and drove her crazy. And she missed the Sean who didn't mind eating takeout, who liked munching popcorn and watching old movies at home, who argued with her over the merits of doing the Sunday crosswords in ink, who raced bikes with her in the park, who thought it was fun to sit in the dark and watch a good rainstorm. But most of all, most of all, she missed the Sean who made her feel beautiful even when she knew she wasn't because he wanted her...wanted her as no one else ever had. Or at least he had wanted her. That he no longer did was painfully evident by the simple fact that he hadn't made love with her once during the past week.

He wanted to end things and was pulling back from her, trying to let her down gently because he didn't want to hurt her. But he was too late, she admitted, pressing the heel of her hand against her heart to ease the pain. She'd thought she'd known heartache before because her heart had ached

when her daddy had left her and her mother. It had ached
again when her mother divorced her stepfather, and twice
more after that when men she'd thought cared about her
had proved they hadn't. But she realized now that she'd
never known the meaning of the word *heartache*. Probably
because she'd never truly loved anyone before—not the
way she loved Sean. But she knew the true meaning of
both words now...because she loved Sean, and because she
loved him, her heart felt as though it was breaking in two.

She squeezed her eyes shut against the tears prickling.
No tears. She'd promised herself at the outset that she
wouldn't make things uncomfortable for him or do anything to jeopardize their friendship. He meant too much to
her to risk losing his friendship, too. Besides, she didn't
want him to feel guilty. He didn't deserve that. She'd
known what she was doing when she began the affair with
him. She'd known from the first that their time together as
lovers would be temporary, that it would come to an end
eventually. She'd told herself all those things, and she'd
been so sure she was prepared. But now...now knowing it
was over was so much worse than she'd ever dreamed it
would be.

One tear sneaked out. She sniffed and swiped it aside.
A summer cold, she told herself when a second tear fell.
When yet another tear slid down her cheek, she curled up
on the couch and blamed it on the fact that she was so
tired. Hugging a throw pillow to her breast, she bit back a
sob.

Had she honestly believed she could make love to him
and walk away unscathed when it was over? It didn't matter
that he didn't love her or that he would never find anyone
who loved him the way she did. But it was time to end it.
To drag things out would only prove more painful for her,
and burden Sean with the guilt of knowing that he'd broken

her heart. Neither was an option. Which meant she would
have to be the one to end it.

Another wave of exhaustion swamped her, and she
clutched the pillow closer, wishing it was Sean. She'd tell
him tonight, Katie decided. Tonight after they came back
from dinner, she would tell him that she wanted to end their
affair. He would understand, Katie told herself. He'd probably even be grateful.

Four hours later Sean didn't appear to be the least bit
grateful. The man was flat-out mad. He glared at her from
the bar in his living room, where he insisted they have a
nightcap. "You care to run that by me again?" Fury blazed
in his eyes, turning them to the color of a winter sky. "Only
this time skip all the bull about friendship and respect, and
just tell me straight-out what you're trying to say."

Katie sighed and wished, yet again, that she didn't feel
so tired—not when she needed all the nerve and energy she
could muster to be able to do this. "What I'm trying to say
is that these past few weeks with you have been...well, the
word *wonderful* hardly seems adequate. You're an incredible lover, Fitzpatrick." Her jaw ached as she forced her
lips to smile.

"I'll never forget, ever, what the two of us have shared."
She sucked in a breath, struggled to keep her voice even
while inside she was dying. "But we both knew when
we...when we..."

"When we what, Katie? Had sex? Hopped in the sack?
Jumped each other's bones?" he offered, his voice bitter,
his expression harsh, as he stormed across the room to her.
He grabbed her by the shoulders, jerked her against him
and savaged her with his mouth. "Just for the record, why
don't you satisfy my curiosity and tell me which one of
those accurately describes what it was for you?"

She pushed at his chest, and he released her. She trembled, shuddered at the hatred in his eyes as he looked at her. Hugging her arms about herself, Katie rubbed her hands up and down her arms where his fingers had bitten into her skin. Sheer will kept her standing, kept her gaze level with his. "For me it was lovemaking. I thought of you as my friend, Sean. My friend who became my lover. And now that we're no longer lovers, I was hoping…I am hoping that we can still be friends."

"Friends?" He all but spit the word at her. "I've slept with you. Made love to you. Touched and tasted every inch of your body. You expect me to go back to being just your friend?"

"I had hoped—"

"You think it's that easy for me? You decide you don't want me anymore, that you don't care about me anymore, and just like that—" he snapped his fingers "—we go back to being friends?"

Confused, her head spinning, Katie tried to make sense of what he was saying. "I didn't say I didn't want you anymore or that I didn't care about you. I do. I'll always care about you. You're my best friend."

"You want to call it quits? Fine. But keep your damn friendship, sweetheart, because I don't want it. I don't need it. And I sure as hell don't need you."

Katie swallowed. She blinked hard, refusing to let him see her cry, even though if he'd put a knife through her heart it would have been less painful. She forced her chin up a notch. "I'm sorry you feel that way, Sean. I had hoped—"

"I don't give a damn what you hoped," he told her, raw fury stamped in the taut lines of his face, the fists at his sides. "You know where the door is. Why don't you use it, and get the hell out of my life?"

Pain, sharp and vicious, sliced through her as he gave her his back. Her head buzzed, and she pressed a shaky hand to her breast as the room started to spin. Sheer will had her putting one foot in front of the other and moving toward the door.

Please, please don't let me break in front of him. Let me get through the door first. When her fingers closed around the doorknob, she thought her prayers had been answered. She dragged in a breath and pulled the door open. Then the world went from a fuzzy gray to black. Her knees buckled. And as she slid to the floor, the last thing she heard was Sean shouting her name.

Eleven

"Katie! Oh, my God, Katie! I'm sorry. I'm sorry, baby. I didn't mean it. You want to be friends? We'll be friends," he told her, rambling like a madman as he cradled her limp body against him. Scared spitless, he rocked her, kissed her, pleaded with her to say something. Anything.

When she stirred, relief washed through him like a storm. "Come on, baby. Open your eyes for me," he begged, his hands shaking as he brushed the hair away from her pale face.

"Sean?" she whispered.

"I'm right here, love. I'm right here, and I'm sorry. I swear I didn't mean any of it," he said, willing to tell her anything, promise her anything, so long as she was all right. Her eyes fluttered, opened, and the sick fear that had turned the blood in his veins to ice began to thaw.

"W-what happened?" she asked, shaking her head as though to clear it.

"What happened?" he repeated, his voice breaking. "You fainted and damn near scared me half to death. That's what happened," he shouted, because fear still had him by the throat. Then he clutched her to his chest and apologized again for yelling. The woman had ripped his heart out. Ripped the thing clean out of him, and then she'd jumped on it with both feet. She'd hurt him, hurt like nothing and no one ever could. And he loved her so much that he'd almost gone after her and begged her to stay. In that moment he'd actually hated her, hated himself because loving her had made him weak. So he'd turned his back on her and reached for the bottle of scotch. So what does she do? She goes and faints on him and scares ten years off his life. He'd forgotten all about the scotch he'd planned to drown himself in and the fact that she'd just dumped him like yesterday's garbage. He loved her, and it just ripped him, really ripped at him, to see her hurt.

"That's impossible," she informed him as she struggled to sit up. "I never faint."

"Yeah? Well, you sure do a hell of an imitation." He knew he was yelling again, didn't mean to, but couldn't seem to stop. He clawed a hand through his hair. A little more color had come into her cheeks, but not much. Her face was still the color of chalk. "Don't move. Let me get my keys, and then I'll take you to the hospital."

She grabbed his arm when he started to rise. "Sean, I don't need a hospital. I'm all right."

"You think fainting is okay? Well, let me tell you, it's not." He swiped a hand over his face, cursed the nerves that were still so close to the surface.

"I mean it, Sean. I'm okay."

"You don't know that. You're not a doctor."

"Neither are you," she reminded him.

"Yeah. But I know you're not yourself," he told her,

wanting to believe that, needing to believe that she hadn't really meant all those things she'd told him tonight. "You've been acting strange for the past week."

"I've been **acting** strange?"

"That's **right**." She was looking at him as if he'd lost his mind. He **didn't** blame her. He felt as if he had. All he knew was that he wasn't leaving her alone tonight. Scooping her up, he kicked the front door shut and started for his bedroom.

"What…where are you taking me?"

"To bed." When she started to protest, he huffed out a breath. "To sleep, Katie. I want you where I can keep an eye on you until I can get you to a doctor in the morning."

"That's absurd. I just got a little light-headed. Nothing's wrong with me. I don't need a doctor. Now, put me down so I can go home."

"Forget it," he told her, and walked into his bedroom. The room still smelled like her, despite the fact that she hadn't been in it or in his bed for nearly a week. A really dumb move on his part, he was beginning to think. Things had been going a lot better between them *before* he'd decided to be so damn noble and court her, try to get her to fall in love with him. He sat her on the edge of the bed and yanked back the comforter.

"This is crazy. I'm telling you there's nothing wrong with me," she informed him and started to get up.

Sean placed his hand on her head and gently pushed her back down. "Crazy or not, you're staying here tonight, and tomorrow you're going to see a doctor."

"Sean—"

"It's not up for discussion, Katie." He pulled off her shoes, slid down the zipper on the back of her dress. When she clutched the top to her breasts, Sean sighed. "Katie, I've already seen you naked more times than I can count.

If I were an artist, I could paint your body from memory. Now either you take off that dress, or I'll do it for you.''

She glared at him, then eased the dress down. ''Satisfied?''

''Not by a long shot,'' he said grimly. And he wouldn't be satisfied, not until he figured out what he'd done wrong and fixed it. Once she was settled in the bed and had the sheet and comforter hiked up to her chin, his heart began to beat easier. Unable to resist, he brushed his fingers down her cheek, then stood and moved to the other side of the bed. After turning off the light, he stripped off his clothes, crawled under the covers and reached for her.

''Sean,'' she started to protest.

''I'm not an animal, Katie. I just want to hold you.'' She allowed him to settle her beside him, their bodies spooned about each other, her legs tangled with his, her bottom tucked against his manhood. ''Try to get some sleep,'' he whispered, pressed a kiss to the back of her head and closed his eyes.

But sleep evaded him. How could he sleep with the remnants of fear and fury still choking him? How could he sleep when all he wanted to do was turn her in his arms, kiss her, make love to her until she couldn't think, wouldn't ever think, about leaving him again?

She pressed her bottom against him, and Sean bit back a groan. He'd told her he wasn't an animal, but he felt like one, because holding her wasn't enough. Would never be enough. He wanted to claim her body, to claim her heart, her very soul—the way she had claimed his. She shifted in his arms, and his fingers brushed her breast. Sean trembled. Sweat broke out across his brow, despite the coolness of the room. When she stirred again, and her breast filled his palm, the air backed up into his lungs. No way was he going to be able to keep his promise to her if he stayed in this bed, he realized. Lifting his arm, he started to ease away.

"Sean."

At the husky sound of her voice saying his name, Sean prayed to the almighty for strength. "Go back to sleep, Katie."

She turned then, her head on his shoulder, her mouth a breath away from his. "Where are you going?"

"To sleep on the couch."

"Why?"

Frustrated, angry with himself because he wanted her so much, he snapped, "Because I can't lie next to you and not want you. Satisfied?"

"Not by a long shot," she said, mimicking his earlier response, her lips curving in a smile. Hope sprang up full-grown inside him, and he laughed out loud. But then she reached for him, pulled his mouth to hers, and laughter was the last thing on his mind.

Faster than a heartbeat, he fastened his mouth to hers. Finally he forced himself to come up a moment for air. "Are you sure you're up to this? That you're all right?"

"I'm fine."

"Thank God," he muttered, and swooped down for another kiss. She wrapped her arms around him, and he thought he would explode with the sheer joy of having her hold him. But within moments, holding and kissing her wasn't nearly enough. He stripped off her slip. Grateful that she hadn't worn a bra, he paused to pay homage to her breasts. "I know we need to talk," he murmured as he tasted his way down her belly, relieved her of her panties. He slid a finger inside, and found her wet and warm and ready. "There are so many things I want to tell you, need to explain to you. And I swear, we will talk—later," he told her as he pressed his mouth to the inside of her thigh, veered south and kissed her again.

"Later," she repeated as he spread her legs and kissed her center. "Please," she murmured, arching her back, lifting her hips. She moaned. "Stop...no, don't stop." Then the fingers fisting in his hair pulled him up to her, dragged his mouth back to hers.

Sean broke free a moment, sucked in a lungful of air. "Katie—" He meant to tell her he loved her, planned to tell her. But then those busy fingers of hers streaked down his chest and closed in a fist around him. He shuddered. The words remained stuck in his throat. The ability to speak flew right out of his head, and he drove himself into Katie and took them both tumbling over the edge.

Later, much, much later, as he held her sleeping in his arms, he kissed her temple and whispered the words aloud. There would be plenty of time to tell her, to talk to her, in the morning, he told himself. Yawning, sleep pulling at him, he closed his eyes.

He would have sworn he'd barely closed his eyes when the ringing of the phone dragged him out of a sound sleep. He reached over, grabbed the receiver beside the bed. "What?"

"Her water broke!"

Recognizing his younger brother's anxious voice, Sean said, "Ryan?" He rubbed at his eyes, glanced at the clock on the nightstand that read a few minutes past five. Easing out of the bed so as not to wake Katie, he slipped out of the bedroom with the portable phone to his ear and shut the door.

"Oh, jeez," Ryan all but screamed in his ear. "Clea's having...the hospital. We're on our way to the baby. Call Mom and Pop." Then the phone went dead. He stared at the phone another minute, stifled another yawn and then, as he dialed his parents home, went into the kitchen and put on coffee.

Ten minutes later he'd dressed, chugged down a cup of coffee, called Michael, and had just taken another frantic call from Ryan, asking him to bring Clea's bag to the hospital. The poor fellow was so nervous, he apparently couldn't think straight. Having fallen in love with Katie, he was beginning to understand how his brother felt. Sensing her presence, Sean looked up and saw Katie standing in the doorway, a sheet wrapped around her.

"I thought I heard the phone," she told him, staring at him out of those big brandy-colored eyes.

Love for her tightened like a fist around his heart. He'd wanted to tell her he loved her and to ask her to marry him this morning. He didn't want to do either and rush out on her. "It was Ryan. Clea's gone into labor. I just finished letting the rest of the family know. Ryan forgot the bag Clea packed for the hospital. I've got to swing by his place, pick it up and take it to them at the hospital."

"If you give me a minute to get dressed, I'll go with you."

"All right," he agreed, because he wanted her with him.

"Think I could have a sip of that coffee first?"

"It'll cost you a kiss," he teased.

She was all sass as she made her way toward him, swishing and swaying her hips. She gave him a chaste peck on the cheek and took the cup from him.

"Not so fast, Malloy. That coffee's going to cost you a lot more—"

Shoving the cup at him, she clutched a hand to her mouth and raced to the bathroom and began to wretch. When the worst of it was over, he lifted her from the floor and took her back to bed on legs that had gone weak. He felt so

damn helpless and scared. "Sean, let me up. I want to go
with you to the hospital."

"Not on your life." He bathed her face with a wet cloth,
then placed another on her forehead. "I'll call Michael and
have him pick up the bag for Clea and Ryan."

"But—"

"No buts. You've got a stomach virus or something. You
want to go around a new baby and risk it catching something from you?"

"No."

But Michael had already gone, and since cell phones
were forbidden in the hospital, he couldn't reach him. "I
can't reach anyone, and no one's answering the page in the
waiting room."

She touched his arm. "You go ahead. I'll be fine. I'm
already feeling better." When he hesitated, she said,
"Go!"

"All right," he agreed reluctantly, but consoled himself
with the fact that she did have some color in her face again.
"But you're still going to the doctor. In fact, why don't
you give me your doctor's name? I'll make an appointment,
and when I get back I'll take you."

"Sean, I can make my own doctor's appointment. Now
go to the hospital and call me and let me know what Clea
has."

He swooped down and gave her a hard kiss. "When I
get back, we need to have that talk."

"Well, Katie, I think we can safely rule out a stomach
virus," Dr. Virginia Ramsey told her in the examining
room a few hours later. "You're pregnant."

"Pregnant," Katie repeated, a thrill of excitement running through her at the doctor's confirmation of her sus-
picions following the morning's events. "Are you sure?"

"I'm positive," she assured her, a gleam in her hazel eyes.

"I can hardly believe it." Katie brought her trembling fingers to her mouth. A baby, she thought, joy bubbling inside her. She was going to have a baby. Sean's baby. "H-how far along am I?"

"My estimate is you're about six weeks."

Six weeks. Six weeks meant she'd gotten pregnant that first night with Sean. A flush stole up her neck as she recalled how daring she'd been, taking the condom from him, tearing the packet open with her teeth. Had she nicked the sheath in her excitement? Probably, she decided.

"I take it this is good news?"

"Oh, yes. It's very good news," Katie responded.

"Then let me be the first to offer you congratulations."

"Thank you," Katie whispered.

Dr. Ramsey squeezed her shoulder. "Now why don't you go ahead and get dressed and then come into my office. I'm going to give you a prescription for some prenatal vitamins."

Fifteen minutes later with her prescription in hand, Katie practically floated out of the medical building. A smile on her face, she pressed her fingers to her stomach where the new life was already growing inside her. She was going to have a baby. Not just any baby, but her and Sean's baby. Drunk with excitement, she wanted to scream the news to the world. She was going to be a mother.

And Sean was going to be a father. She sobered instantly. How would Sean feel about a baby? After what had started out to be the most miserable evening of her life, she'd humiliated herself by fainting. Katie grinned as she recalled how everything shifted after that. Sean streaking across the room to her, holding her and rambling a string of apologies. Panic, anger, fear—all that emotion swimming in his eyes had baffled her, made her hope. But the pain in his voice, the need she'd felt trembling through him as he lay beside her had made her turn to him. They'd never gotten around to talking, and she'd held back the words of love in her heart, nearly choking on them, because she hadn't wanted to pressure him to say them in return. But the way he'd kissed her, loved her so tenderly, so completely, all that had been missing were the words.

And if you're wrong? the pesky voice inside her head nagged. *Will he feel obligated, even trapped because of the baby? Do you want him that way?*

She didn't. Starting her car, she eased out of the parking garage and headed for home, anxious to see Sean. As she made the twenty-minute drive, she rehearsed the scene over and over in her mind. She would start out by telling Sean that she loved him, and then she would tell him they were going to have a baby. She played out two endings, preparing herself.

But she hadn't prepared well enough, Katie realized, when she hurried up the stairs to the apartment complex and pulled open the door. Then she saw them—Sean standing in the narrow hallway with Heather in his arms. Her heart stopped beating. Pain and fury slammed through her, wrenching an anguished cry from her lips.

"Katie, wait," Sean yelled, yanking the other woman's arms from around his neck and shoving her away from him.

"No, thanks. I've played this scene before, and I know how it ends."

Heather grabbed Sean's arm. "Let her go, Sean."

He swore, tore the woman's fingers free and started after Katie. "Katie, wait. Let me explain."

But she was already down the stairs, racing for her Jeep. She jammed the key into the ignition and, tires spinning, she sped off down the street. And only when she could no longer see him, did she let the tears fall.

"All right, Molly. Where is she?"

"Where's who?" his cousin replied, all innocence.

"Katie. That's who." In no mood for games, Sean shoved his way into his cousin's apartment and turned on the woman who had guarded Katie's whereabouts for the past five days. He sank to the couch, buried his head in his hands. After that nightmarish scene, he hadn't seen or heard from Katie. She hadn't been to work. She wasn't at her mother's, and he believed the older woman when she said she didn't know where her daughter was. That left Molly, Katie's pal and cohort. She had to know where Katie was. "I'm going out of my mind. Please," he pleaded. "Tell me where she is."

Molly hesitated. "You hurt her pretty bad."

"Don't you think I know that?" he snapped. It clawed at him that he had. If only she had let him explain. He'd come home, anxious to see Katie, to have that talk he should have had the previous night. He wanted to tell her that he loved her, that he wanted to marry her. Only Katie hadn't been the one waiting. Heather had. He'd told Heather it was over weeks ago, that there was someone else in his life now. But the stubborn woman was either thickheaded or simply refused to accept it. He'd tried again to let her down gently, didn't see a point in being nasty. But in a last-ditch effort, the woman had launched herself at him and caught him off guard with that kiss when Katie had walked in. If he lived to be a hundred, he'd never forget that look of betrayal on Katie's face. "Please, Molly. I love her. I've never begged a soul for anything in my life, but I'm begging you now," he told her, and started to drop to his knees.

"Oh, for Pete's sake," his hard-nosed cousin exclaimed, grabbing him by the arm and jerking him to his feet. "She's at the beach staying in a condo that belongs to a friend of mine. But so help me, Sean, you hurt her again, and I swear you'll have me to answer to."

It was a fairy-tale castle fit for a prince and his princess, Katie mused as she sat back on her heels and surveyed her creation. Gathering a handful of sand, she let the grains sift through her fingers.

What a fraud, you are, Katie Malloy. You never did stop believing in those fairy tales, did you? And you thought you'd finally found your prince—Sean. Only you weren't the princess Sean wanted.

But Sean had wanted her, he had loved her at least for a little while, she told herself. She refused to believe she could have been that wrong. It still hurt, but she couldn't regret loving him. How could she, when he'd given her such a precious gift? Their baby. A reminder of what real love was, what it should be. She pressed a hand to her stomach and smiled as she thought of the life growing inside her that represented the love they had shared.

A seagull squawked, dipped to the water's edge and shot back up to the sky. The sun had already begun to slide in the distance, turning the summer sky a dusky blue. She glanced at lovers walking hand in hand, laughing, kissing— at the families gathering their children, beach umbrellas and chairs to make their way home for the day.

She would have to go home soon, Katie told herself. She needed to let Sean know about the baby. Knowing him as she did, he would offer to marry her for the baby's sake. Of course she would refuse. Funny, she thought as she gave the turret on her castle another pat, she was going to get her birthday wish after all. She was going to have a baby, and the amazing thing was that the father would be the first man who had come to mind when she'd made up that silly list of daddy candidates. Sean.

"No wonder I haven't been able to reach you. Your castle doesn't have a phone."

Katie's heart stammered at the familiar voice, and she stared openmouthed as Sean dropped down beside her in the sand. Finally she mastered her tongue. "Molly told you."

"Don't blame her. I tortured her until she gave you up."

"I doubt that even torture would make your cousin do anything she didn't want to do."

He took a handful of sand and packed it around the castle wall. "Another Fitzpatrick trait. We're a stubborn lot," he told her. "Sometimes we're too stubborn to see what's been staring us in the face most of our lives."

Katie searched his face, saw the anxiety in his eyes. "I'm sorry I ran out on you the way I did."

"Oh, love. I'm the one who's sorry about so many things. I'm sorry for not having that talk with you sooner. For that thing with Heather. It's not what it looked like. I—"

She dropped the fistful of sand, not wanting him to tell her he was in love with the other woman. "Sean, you don't have to explain."

"Yes, I do. And this time I'm going to finish. I'd told Heather weeks ago that there was someone else in my life, that I wasn't interested in her. I tried to let her down gently, but either she didn't get the message or she didn't want to accept it. She just showed up that day, and that kiss was her final shot at me. But I've told her in no uncertain terms that she has no place in my life. There's only one woman I want in my life, and that woman is you."

Katie swallowed, hope and joy kicking her heart. "Sean,

there's something I need to tell you first. I was going to tell you when I got back.''

"No, I need to tell you what I planned to say that morning before Ryan called, and for once you're going to let me finish. I love you, Katie Malloy. I think I've loved you from the first time you beaned me with that snowball. It's just taken me twenty years to figure it out.''

"I love you, too,'' she told him, unable to keep the smile from her face.

"I'm sorry, love, but I've got to do this.'' He kissed her then, cupping her face with sand-dusted hands and hugged her to him. "I love you. I know I'm not Prince Charming or a knight in shining armor, but I love you with all my heart, and I don't want to live without you. I want you to marry me.''

"Oh, Sean.'' She hugged him tight, then eased away. "There's still something I have to tell you. Remember how I made up that list of daddy candidates.''

"Katie—''

She pressed a finger to his lips. "I'm pregnant.''

He went stock-still. His face filled with shock, and then his mouth split into a grin. "You're sure?''

She nodded her head and waited.

"Then I guess we're going to need a bigger castle, won't we? Come on, Princess. It's time to go home.''

* * * * *

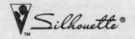

If you enjoyed what you just read,
then we've got an offer you can't resist!

Take 2 bestselling love stories FREE!

Plus get a FREE surprise gift!

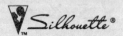

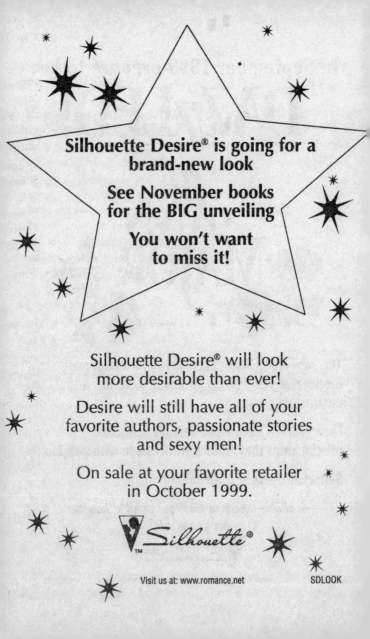

Silhouette Desire® is going for a brand-new look

See November books for the BIG unveiling

You won't want to miss it!

Silhouette Desire® will look more desirable than ever!

Desire will still have all of your favorite authors, passionate stories and sexy men!

On sale at your favorite retailer in October 1999.

Silhouette®